Contents

CHAPTER ONE 4

CHAPTER TWO 19

CHAPTER THREE..33

CHAPTER FOUR 40

CHAPTER FIVE 53

CHAPTER SIX 64

CHAPTER SEVEN..79

CHAPTER EIGHT 92

CHAPTER NINE 110

CHAPTER TEN..121

CHAPTER ELEVEN 129

CHAPTER TWELVE 135

CHAPTER THIRTEEN 148

CHAPTER FOURTEEN...154

CHAPTER FIFTEEN 159

CHAPTER SIXTEEN 176

CHAPTER SEVENTEEN 194

CHAPTER EIGHTEEN 213

CHAPTER NINETEEN..236

CHAPTER TWENTY 245

CHAPTER TWENTY-ONE 260

CHAPTER TWENTY-TWO 277

~ About the Author ~...291

"You sealed your demise when you took
what was mine."
~Bullet for My Valentine "Waking the Demon"

CHAPTER ONE

Haley Hawthorne straightened her pencil skirt and
glanced at her cell phone for the hundredth time. Frowning,
she slid into the driver's seat of her little black Porsche. Her
boyfriend, Damian, hadn't come home last night. He
usually called if he was going to be late, but she hadn't
heard from him. She tried to shake off the uneasy feeling.
Her brother, Adam, had just taken over as head of
Adversus, the government agency Damian worked for. He
would have told her if something went wrong with Damian
and Noah's mission.

She waved at the burly security guard as she drove
out of the parking garage of the Hawthorne office building.
He nodded back without a smile. That one in particular had

a constant scowl. Actually, all the giant men on the security team Damian hired for her building seemed permanently angry.

Sitting in heavy traffic in downtown Seattle, she pressed the call button on the car stereo. Her cousin Ginger answered right away.

"Have you heard from Damian?" Ginger sounded as desperate as Haley felt.

"No. Nothing from Noah?"

"I called him this morning when I woke up to an empty house. Straight to voicemail. I've been on the couch all day just staring at my phone. I feel like a loser."

Haley raked her fingers through her long red wavy curls. "Do you think something happened?"

Ginger paused. "I kinda want to go poke Adam for information. I've been calling him too. No answer."

Since his promotion with Adversus, Adam had moved back into their childhood home, a multi-level brick mansion built into the side of a hill in North Seattle they referred to as the Castle. He would certainly have an update on Damian and Noah's whereabouts.

"I'll meet you there," Haley said and disconnected the call.

Dozens of random cars lined the long winding driveway that led to her former home. Inside the Castle, loud music vibrated the walls. She hadn't lived there since her college years, but the classic old-world décor remained unchanged. Adam had turned the place into quite a party house since he'd taken over as the sole tenant. Laughter exploded from the main sitting room as Haley walked by. She searched the sea of unknown faces all around her with a sharp anxiety in her stomach.

Six years earlier, she'd escaped from Damian's uncle Raden, the brother of Satan, who'd kept her in Hell as his personal sex slave for three months. The fear of being captured again still loomed over her head.

Firm hands pulled her into a dark office, and she wrenched free from their hold.

Talis flicked on a lamp. "Didn't mean to scare you."

Haley's pulse shot up. The last time she'd seen Talis here, Damian had nearly beaten him to death in a jealous brawl, unhinging Talis's jaw in the process. It appeared the Healers had fixed Talis up properly, leaving no scars on his perfect olive skin.

"I haven't talked to you in a while." He dragged a hand through his thick dark hair as his gaze wandered down her body. "How are you doing?"

Folding her arms across herself, she glanced away from his groping stare.

"I know I fucked up." Talis slumped his brawny shoulders. His deep brown eyes seemed sincere. "I got pissed off when I saw you with Damian."

"Why?" She tightened her arms around her waist. The only history she had with Talis was a bad memory of him rejecting her upon seeing her scarred stomach.

"I wanted another chance with you." He studied her face and moved closer. His gaze settled on her breasts and his voice went husky. "I think you're sexy, Hales."

He reached for her chin, and she leaned away, then eased around his massive frame.

"I'm with Damian, you know that. I think he made that pretty clear to you." She turned and grasped the doorknob.

Talis backed her up against the door. "How can you be with him?" He brushed his knuckles along the branded R underneath her clothes and a shiver ran through her. "After what his family did to you."

"I'm in love with him." She pulled the door open and darted out into the hall, hoping he wouldn't follow, but he grabbed her elbow, leaning toward her ear.

"Can you listen for a second?"

She flinched away from him. "Sorry," she mumbled and started down the hallway.

Adam stood at the end of the hall. He'd cut his typically shaggy brown hair, and his new look was all business. He crossed his arms, deep in conversation with Noah.

Her stomach tensed when she caught Damian's hard gaze. His piercing green eyes, typically radiant emeralds, glimmered almost black in the dim light, and his shaded jaw was clenched shut.

He ran his hand over his short buzzed dark hair and shifted his attention to Adam. Her heartbeat thudded faster.

Talis gripped her arm. "Hang on a second."

She spun toward him. "Don't touch me."

He let go, drawing back from her. "Whatever."

Her shoulders loosened as he walked away, and she took a steadying breath.

She turned back and halted. Damian's muscles were rigid beneath his tight white T-shirt and veins bulged under his black tattoos along his forearms as he approached her. Speechless, she caught the grave expression on his handsome face.

"Are you okay?" she asked.

Towering over her, he grasped her wrist and pulled her toward the staircase. Chills ran through her as she let him lead her down the stairs. He kept his dominant hold on her and brought her into her old bedroom.

Damian crowded her back against the door as he shut it, pinning her against it. He crashed his mouth into hers and tingles erupted through her entire body at the contact. He parted her lips with his insistent tongue, grazing it along hers in her mouth while he ran his large palm up the front of her collared shirt, fondling and squeezing her breast.

She broke away from his hot kiss. "Are you gonna punish me?"

His eyes darkened, and he reached behind her and turned the key, locking the door. "Do you deserve a punishment, naughty witch?" His deep voice was rugged.

"No." Her breath sped up in anticipation.

With a smirk, he grabbed her hips and walked her backward toward the window, then turned her away from him and pressed her down over the white dresser. "Why were you alone with Talis?" He inched her tight black skirt upward, revealing her lacy underwear.

"He wanted to apologize."

Damian skimmed his rough palm up along her bare inner thigh, and her clit twitched, yearning for more.

He took his hand away. "Did he touch you?" Sliding his fingers through her long cinnamon waves, he drew her hair back away from her neck.

"No."

He closed his fist around her hair, leaning against her back, and dragged his teeth along her throat. "Did you miss me?"

"Yes." Her nipples stiffened beneath her silk top, and she closed her eyes. "I've been calling you."

"We lost our phones during the mission." He grasped her panties in his fist, stretching them, and the lace strained between her legs.

She pressed her ass against the front of his jeans. Arousal spread through her as she felt the hardness behind his zipper. "I was so worried about you."

He drew her upright and released her hair. His stubble scraped her neck as he ran his tongue over her ear. "You know you don't ever have to worry, baby."

Her vision dimmed, and she leaned back against him. "I can't help it."

Damian pressed his face into her throat with a soft groan and groped his hands along her breasts. "I fucking missed you too, angel."

He took one of her filmy scarves she used to wear in college from a hook on the wall, and her pulse pumped faster as he pulled her arms behind her back. He slid the thin material around her elbows, tightening it until she couldn't move her arms, and tied it in place.

He turned her to face him. With her arms pinned tightly behind her, she held onto the edge of the dresser as he grasped her collar and ripped her shirt open. Buttons scattered and he reached into his pocket.

He withdrew a silver knife and opened it. Her eyes widened.

She tried not to breathe as he slid the cold blade beneath the lace covering her breast. The sharp steel drifted toward her stiff nipple, and she forced her erratic breath to steady.

Damian cut through the dainty lace and ripped it apart, exposing her breasts, and her pink nipples hardened painfully. He lowered the knife, and she took a deep breath.

He ran his devouring mouth along her breast and caught her nipple between his teeth, then sucked on it. She parted her legs as sensation flooded through her clit. He crouched to his knees, staring at the transparent lace covering her sex, and slowly stroked the edge of the blade up her inner thigh.

She opened her mouth, trembling as the metal point grazed underneath her panties. He swept it along her freshly waxed lips and fear prickled across her skin. She gasped softly, trying not to shiver as he skimmed the steel edge along her slit.

He sliced through the thin fabric, then grabbed her panties with his masculine hand and tore them away from her.

Completely bare, she worked to keep her legs steady as he continued to caress the edge of the knife across her pussy, and her clit pulsed with desire.

Turning the knife, he grasped the blade and slid the cold metal handle inside her. Her mouth dropped open as he pushed the thick steel in and out of her, the raised ridges of the grip teasing her G-spot.

He pulled the knife out, folded and pocketed it, then glanced up at her with smoldering emerald eyes. "Tell me when you're close."

She leaned her head back, gripped with desire and frustrated by his words. He loved to torment her until she was begging him to let her come.

He forked his tongue into two tips and grazed it between her legs. His soft lips and scratchy stubble against her sensitive sex brought her quickly to the edge of climax, and she bit her lip with a moan.

"I'm close..." She squeezed her eyes shut as he pulled his perfect mouth away.

Panting, she gripped the dresser behind her, and he skidded his fingertips all over her inner thighs. His feathery tongue drifted along her pussy lips, avoiding her needy center.

Haley opened her legs wider, showing him her desperate clit. "Please."

She breathed a soft moan as he dragged his velvety tongue across it.

He pushed his thick fingers past her entrance and spread them apart, then stroked them inside her while he gently licked.

She dug her nails into the wood, whimpering at his torture. "I'm close."

Damian withdrew his hand and shoved her skirt higher. He glided his tongue up along her stomach and trailed his mouth across her scar.

She could hardly breathe. The urgent need between her legs was too intense. "Please touch me..."

He closed his mouth over her breast with a low growl and sucked hard. His fingers swept across her clitoris and she melted, instantly ready to come.

"I'm so close," she mumbled, helpless as tingles rushed through her body.

He pulled his hand away and slapped her wet pussy. She jerked at the contact, craving more. She widened her legs, giving herself to him as he smacked her clit again.

Her body tensed up as she tried to control the overwhelming urge.

Damian roughly grasped her inner thigh. "You don't come until I let you, Haley."

Her vision blurred as his hand slipped upward between her legs. "Baby... Please let me come."

"Turn around." His low voice was laced with his own desire.

She swiftly obeyed his gruff command. He bent her forward over the dresser, and she pressed her cheek to the wood. His calloused fingertips raked across her clit, and she jolted.

He opened his belt buckle, and her pussy ran wet at the sound of the leather sliding through his belt loops as she waited for the erotic sting of his belt.

He grazed the leather strap across her ass and down along her clit. He tapped it between her legs, and she flinched, then spread her legs wider.

"Good girl." Damian was breathing harder. He swept his fingertips along her ass, then spanked her. Groaning, he grabbed her ass with a firm grip. "You're so fucking sexy, Haley." From behind, he pressed the front of his jeans against her exposed pussy and Haley rubbed herself along his bulge, desperate for his big, punishing cock.

Tightening her fists against her lower back, she forced herself to stop. "I'm about to come," she whimpered.

Damian stepped back and whipped his belt between her legs. She shivered at the sharp sensation. He rubbed her clit with his strong fingers, and she cried out.

"I'm so close, baby, please …"

He struck her pussy with the belt again, and she widened her legs, tilting toward the licking strokes.

"You're gonna make me come, Damian…"

He lowered his belt. Reaching toward her face, he brushed his knuckles along her cheek, and she leaned her face toward his tender touch. His voice was gentle. "How do you want to come, angel? On my belt or my cock?"

She swallowed, teeming with sensual desire as he glided the harsh leather through her pussy.

"Your cock. Please, I need your cock." She used a desperate tone.

He dropped his belt on the dresser and quickly opened his jeans. Pleasure melted through her as he pressed the tip of his cock against her throbbing clit. His loving hands caressed a path along her bound arms, and he gripped her wrists as he shoved his huge cock inside her.

She breathed a moan and relaxed against the wood. Welcoming his pounding thrusts, she pushed back against him.

"Please, baby, I need to come." Her quiet voice jerked as he plunged deep inside.

Groaning, he gathered her hair behind her head, pulling it as he drove his cock in deeper, then reached down and swept his fingertips across her swollen clit. "Sexy witch... You can come."

She closed her eyes as her shocking climax tore through her, releasing around his enormous cock in long, delicious spasms. Damian emptied his hot cum inside her, circling his fingertips over her clitoris as he slid in and out of her, and she moaned at the delicious sensations.

Her body felt numb, and she rested against the dresser, her heart pounding. Waiting for her pulse to calm, she focused on steadying her breath.

Still buried inside her, Damian untied the scarf and massaged along her arms with his warm hands.

A smile spread across her lips as he withdrew from her, and she reveled in the relaxing bliss for a few moments, then lazily moved upright.

"How did you lose your phone?" She unzipped her skirt and inched it down to the floor, then slipped off her torn blouse.

Stepping out of her high heels, she glanced up at him. His gaze slid along her naked curves, settling at the apex of her thighs as he buttoned his jeans.

With a hint of a smile, she leaned against the dresser. "Are you gonna answer me?"

He traced his thumb along her rough scar and cleared his throat. "We got captured," he muttered.

Her heart stopped, and she struggled to take a breath. "Are you hurt?"

Damian kept his gaze on her marked skin. "A few bruises, nothing bad."

He's lying. Tears flooded her eyes without warning. She grasped his T-shirt and drew it upward. Purple and black welts covered his muscled abdomen and deep cuts crisscrossed his body, swollen and angry looking. They must have tortured him with an enchanted weapon.

Her stomach tightened into knots as her throat closed up, and she lowered his shirt back down.

Because he was immortal, Damian healed quickly, but she couldn't stand to see him wounded. Tears spilled down her cheeks, and she brushed them away.

"You said I didn't have to worry."

"I meant it, baby, I'll always find a way to make it home to you." He touched her chin and lifted it. "You're the only thing on my mind when I'm out there."

She drifted closer to him and buried her face against his shoulder, fighting a fresh wave of tears. "I love you."

Damian wrapped his arms around her in a powerful hold and groaned. "I love you, angel." He trailed gentle kisses up her neck and along the side of her face. "You never have to be afraid of losing me."

CHAPTER TWO

"Welcome to Hell." Noah adjusted his collar in front of the mirror in Damian's living room. "How'd you get roped into going to a fucking fashion auction?"

Damian leaned against his front door, his mouth set in a grim line. This wasn't about to become a regular thing, but he could make it through one night for Haley.

"At least this one has food." Noah straightened his tie. "The one next week is at an art gallery. All they've got is champagne."

"Can't wait." Damian took a drink of his whiskey and glanced up at the empty staircase.

Noah plopped down into a chair. "Yeah, wait till you're planning your goddamn wedding. Ginger's thought about everything. All the way down to the napkins. Haley's probably the same way."

Damian set his drink down, shaking his head. "She doesn't care about that shit."

Noah snorted. "That's what she's making you think now. She's probably hiding wedding spreadsheets like porn on her computer."

Haley appeared at the top of the stairs, fumbling with her bracelet, and started down the steps. Her dress looked expensive, light-mint filmy fabric ran all the way to her ankles with a slit at her thigh. He loved when she wore that kind of shit.

She looked in his direction and faltered on the last step, gazing over his dark-gray suit. Her high heels barely tapped the marble as she gravitated toward him. Her tight dress wrapped around her curves, pushing up her perfect tits.

She bit her bottom lip and ran her palm along his tie. Her sweet voice echoed in his head. *"I kind of want to get on my knees right now."*

The thought sent a ripple of pleasure through his cock, and he moved his hands to her waist.

Ginger headed down the stairs, saying something to Noah.

Damian clutched the delicate silk of Haley's dress, ready to rip it off her, and replied into her mind. *"In front of our friends?"*

"Are we taking separate cars?" Noah called to him as he slid on his jacket.

Haley glanced over at Noah. "Yeah."

Damian caught her chin, then glided his tongue across her lower lip. She tasted like sin, and he needed more. Driving his tongue into her soft mouth, he pulled her closer.

He slid his hand down to her ass, and she stiffened a little in his arms. He forced himself to let go of her.

Blushing, she pressed her gorgeous rosy lips together. He couldn't help but stare at them, hungry for her, but he stepped back, shackling his desperate lust.

"See you guys there." Noah draped his arm across Ginger's shoulders as he pulled the door open.

Haley turned to the table by the entryway and slipped the folded silver knife he'd given her into a small silk purse. Sexy little soldier, always armed like he taught her. The steel knife was engraved with ancient spells, meant to destroy supernatural beings. It provided peace of mind against the monsters who'd imprisoned her in Hell six years ago.

He swept his fingers underneath the tiny strap of her dress and guided her toward the door. She wouldn't need to fear his uncle much longer, Damian had been working with Adam to assemble an attack against Raden.

With a little smile, she clutched her skirt, lifting it a few inches as they headed down the front steps. "I've never seen you wear a suit before."

He pulled open the passenger door of his classic 1970 Chevelle, itching to bend her over the hood. "I only have a few. Never really need to wear them."

Her heated deep-blue gaze wandered down his body, and she let out a quiet breath. "I can't wait to take it off you." She turned and got into the Chevelle, and he shut her door.

His cock pressed against his zipper as he walked to the driver's side. Fuck, it was gonna be a long night.

They arrived at the auction and dinner was served at their table. Eggplant something. Damian pushed it around with his fork. Another trendy person took the podium and spoke in long, drawn-out sentences about designers and summer fashion lines.

Haley moved her chair closer to him. "Are you bored to death yet?"

"No." It was a tremendous lie, but she looked happy.

She glanced down at his plate. "You don't like it?" Her glittery eyes reflected a playful gleam, and he relaxed his muscles.

"I prefer the food I get at home."

Smiling, Haley brought her hand to his lap. "I'll make you one of your favorites for dinner tomorrow."

He set down his fork, suddenly craving only her delicious pussy. He rubbed his mouth as his pulse picked up. Taking a deep breath, he resisted the urge to move her innocent hand to his thickening cock.

Instead, he took hold of her palm and massaged it. Touching her silky skin sent electric tingles through his body, heightening his desperation. He traced his fingers along the tender veins in her wrist, and her hand went limp in his grip. Lifting it to his lips, he gently kissed her palm, then lowered it back to his lap, barely grazing his hardness. She dropped her long lashes and her cheeks flushed pink. He leveled his gaze on her steadily heaving breasts.

With his heartbeat pounding, he leaned in close to her. "I need to fuck you, angel."

She took a soft breath and nodded. Grabbing her little purse, she stood up from her chair.

He could hardly keep his throbbing dick in his pants as they hurried through a busy foyer. He drew her down a secluded hallway, lined with hanging gold-and-crystal chandeliers.

Pressing her against the wall, he fumbled with her dress. His fingers met with thin lace, and he grunted in frustration, gripping her panties in his fist.

"Someone's coming," she whispered and inched her dress down.

Two men approached from the other end of the hall with a steady stride. Damian searched their minds, and they both revealed the same thing: echoing chasms of darkness.

Damian shoved her behind him and snatched his knife from his pocket. Shadows crept around him. He spun as a snarling demon appeared from the black fog, right behind Haley.

Her silk purse hit the floor as she flipped open her silver knife and thrust it into the underside of the demon's chin. The demon vanished into the darkness.

The two men morphed into their true forms, twisted, deformed bodies with serpent-like flesh. They lunged at him from both sides, and Damian dodged their blows. He plunged his knife into one demon's throat as the other one grabbed him from behind. Turning, he sank his blade into the disfigured face, and the demon disappeared in the smoke.

A mass of shadow engulfed Haley as a monstrous demon lurking behind her closed his arms around her small frame. She gripped her knife, struggling to free her arm from his powerful hold.

As she slipped away into the black cloud, Damian latched onto it. They appeared in the familiar lavish surroundings of his uncle Raden's bed chambers. Black velvet drapes hung along the two-story-tall windows in the huge tower. The deep red sky outside cast a dismal glow into the dark space, lit only by eerie candlelight. They had been dragged to Hell.

"Just in time, nephew."

Haley stared up at Raden with wide eyes. Long black hair framed his sharp features. He sneered, his black eyes full of hatred. She appeared so tiny beside the giant adversary looming over her.

Demons swarmed Damian, attacking him from every side, and he blocked their weapons. He stabbed into them, slicing through their scaly bodies to get to her, but they overwhelmed him.

Raden took hold of her dress and ripped it open. He tore off her panties, leaving her stark naked.

Damian's chest tightened into a strained knot. Hardly able to breathe, he pushed forward, fighting the horde of creatures.

Haley gripped her silver knife and swiftly shoved it into Raden's massive groin. His immortal body would heal in a matter of moments, but he gave a satisfying roar of agony.

His uncle snatched her wrist in his giant fist, and she cried out. He wrenched the blade's handle out of her grip and pulled the knife from his crotch. Locking eyes with Damian through the crowd of frantic demons, he plunged the blade between Haley's breasts and dragged it downward.

Damian's heart seized in his chest. She grabbed her gaping wound as she fell forward.

Desperate, Damian overpowered the monsters and slid in front of her, catching her before she hit the black marble.

He couldn't breathe as he helped her hold her bleeding stomach. "Use your powers, Haley. Heal yourself."

"I can't."

A choking pain struck him. She had been stabbed with her own knife, the enchanted gift he'd given her.

"Hold on, baby." He shook his head, panicked at how quickly everything had unraveled.

"I love you." She took a labored breath as the color drained from her face. "I wanted to have your children."

"No, angel... Hold on."

The life left her eyes. Her chest didn't rise with another breath.

His eyes burned with tears, something he didn't know his body could produce, and he held her corpse tightly to his chest. "Don't leave me, Haley. I'll fix this."

But he knew the ancient spells engraved on the knife couldn't be broken. She was dead. There was no way to fix anything.

Numb, he barely heard his uncle's bellowing laughter.

"If your father could see you now."

Gripped with a darkness he couldn't control, Damian spoke his native demonic language of Trinnian, his voice cracking. "Di arak de'erden."

Silence fell over the room. A moment later, Raden jolted as the enormous glass window in his chambers shattered, the frame suddenly filled with a mammoth, scaly creature, leering at him with fire brimming in its mouth.

Damian's dragon was missing a few scales, but it had grown in the many years since he'd seen it. It looked to him for direction as if he were still its master. The creature had remained loyal to him even in his absence. Damian uttered a command in Trinnian, and the monster began to stalk toward his uncle, awaiting Damian's next command.

"Lucifer will never allow this, Damian. Spare yourself from his wrath. Call back your dragon."

A visible shadow of darkness cloaked Damian's body, emanating from within. "Nn ebbeneit ferrough exey."

Raden shrieked as the dragon's fire consumed him. The giant creature held him down and tore his sinewy body into pieces with its piercing teeth.

Carrying her body, Damian climbed on top of the dragon while it feasted. Her eyes, once a vibrant, glittering blue, stared at nothing. He lowered his forehead to her neck, shocked by how cold she already felt.

"I didn't know you wanted children." He swallowed through the pain in his throat. "We can still do that. We'll make you immortal, baby."

Raden had become a gory puddle on the marble, and the dragon turned to the broken window. It glided forward, flying out of the tall tower with Damian on its back.

Surrounded by the dark crimson sky, Damian began to black out, unable to process the crushing agony in his chest. He tightened his hold on her lifeless form and told himself to hold it together. He would bring her back.

He stepped down from his dragon and gave it a nod. The reptile took flight, leaving him standing at the doorway of his childhood home, the dark palace of Hell where his father currently resided. The monsters guarding the doors stepped aside for him, and he carried her bloodied body through the monumental hall.

Satan sat on his throne in a vast, empty room, looking down at him with a knowing grin.

"My son has returned." His voice echoed with a strange sound, oddly high-pitched yet combined with a deep resonating growl. "I see you are exuding my dark power." He gestured one of his four arms to the black shadow surrounding Damian, similar to the one that followed him wherever he went, making his presence known before he arrived.

"Father." Damian dropped to his knees and leaned over Haley's overly pale naked body.

"I knew the witch would bring you back here. The oracles predicted it."

"Help me," he whispered. The foreign-feeling tears fell from his eyes again.

"The witch deserved to die, Damian. Our power is to destroy. I cannot create life."

"You created *me*."

"The life inside you is only darkness. You are not capable of the love you have professed to her."

"Then you can turn back the clock. Give me another chance to save her."

"It is clear I must explain something to you." Lucifer's vibrating vocal chords caused the enormous walls to shake. "The one who carries the golden powers—the queen—has dominion over all other witches. And long before you were created, I found myself obsessed with her. Your witch's mother, Grace. She seduced me, letting me hide in her room, letting me touch her while she slept. When she discovered me one night, I took her by force and made her mine in every way. The queen's powers are alluring, Damian, it's why Raden sent the bloodlings to murder Grace. It's also why he chose her daughter to be his personal slave." He narrowed his snake-like eyes. "It's why you believe yourself to be in love with her."

Damian shook his head. "She's given me countless reasons to love her, father. She belongs with me."

"Why would I grant you anything? My son, the rightful heir to my throne, has chosen to be a soldier for Adversus, an organization devoted to killing my armies. You have disgraced me."

"Raden used an enchanted blade." His heart felt like it was barely pumping, bleeding in his chest. "A blade *I* gave to her. I can't..." He closed his raw eyes, stung with scalding tears. "I can't live without her, father."

"And then you proceeded to kill my brother, your own uncle. I must teach you a lesson, Damian. Your behavior cannot be met with mercy. The queen witch shall remain as she is, I suggest you bury her body before the mortem rats catch the scent of her flesh. They do love to devour the dead."

"Father, please." Damian pressed his face against her body, unable to find any comfort from her cold breasts. "I need her."

"I have heard enough." Lucifer gripped the arms of the throne and showed a smile full of sharp teeth. "We will return to the time before you betrayed me. You will ascend to your rightful place on the throne. You will *never* join Adversus, and therefore, you'll never meet the seductive queen witch. Your life with her will not exist. But because of your sacrifice, your witch shall not die at Raden's hand. Accept the offer or toss her dead body into the Pit."

It wasn't truly a choice. Damian couldn't go on in the devastating darkness. Saving her was the only option he could live with, and if he never had her, at least he wouldn't have to experience the pain of losing her. With a heavy, wounded heart, he looked his father in the eye.

"I'll take the throne."

CHAPTER THREE

"Do you plan to kill Marybelle once you become the dark lord, nephew?" Raden leaned back in his chair with his typical smirk. "Perhaps strap *her* to a torture device for a change?"

The other men seated around the metal table in Raden's chambers snickered. Everyone in Hell was aware their future leader had spent three of his teenaged years as the prisoner of a witch. It made him look weak. Damian was expected to take his revenge on her when he received the supernatural powers of the throne, but it was the furthest thing from his mind. It had been seven years since Raden had saved him from her torture table, and he was content to never think about the sick little witch ever again.

"Well? What is the pixie-witch's fate?"

Damian continued to ignore Raden, grateful when the chamber doors burst open, diverting his uncle's attention.

"Speaking of filthy witches." Raden stood up from his chair, glaring at the slave who the guards dragged across the floor by the enchanted wispy white collar around her neck. She was a curvy young redhead, her cinnamon hair hanging in long layers of wavy curls that covered her face.

The demon holding her collar bowed his head to Raden. "She tried to escape, Master. Killed two of our guards before we caught her."

Raden yanked her over to the table and spread her naked body across it, pressing her face against the metal.

Damian's pulse skyrocketed at the inevitable pain he was about to see inflicted on the pale witch. He didn't like witches. They were able to dominate him with their powers, a strange flaw in his genetic armor. But watching the slaves' unnecessary suffering was not something he enjoyed either. He shifted in his seat as he found himself gazing at the witch's stunning blue eyes and clenched his hands into fists.

Haley kept her cheek on the cold surface and stared ahead at the black tattooed symbols on the man's forearms, resting on the table next to her. Her master, Raden, cruelly wrenched her legs apart while he took off his belt. The men's eyes roamed over her bare skin, covered in deep sores inflicted by Raden's favorite device, his whip. At least his belt just left welts and bruises, the leather whip sliced through her sensitive skin with every stroke. She automatically checked out mentally whenever the real pain began, escaping to another world inside her mind.

Raden was performing for his audience at the table, swinging the belt with powerful smacks, purposefully landing it between her legs where it stung the most. Her eyes welled up with humiliated tears. As the pain began to increase, she suppressed the wild urge to run. She wasn't tied up, but the collar made it impossible to use her powers. She would be instantly overpowered if she tried anything.

She flinched at the smarting pain of the leather and choked out a sob, bringing cheers from the evil men staring at her.

The man with the black tattoos seemed to shift uncomfortably, tensing his muscles, and her gaze drifted up to his face. His eyes were a shocking bright green, iridescent lights in sharp contrast to his dark eyelashes. He held her gaze, and she couldn't look away, furiously biting down on her lip to keep from whimpering as she stared up at him.

He stood quickly, tearing his focus away from her.

"Nephew," Raden called after him, but he was already out in the mansion's hall. The heavy door closed with a slam.

She tried to block out the sharp pain as the beating continued. Raden's nephew. He had locked eyes with her for so long, practically hypnotizing her. He'd appeared a little lost in her gaze as well. Just before he'd stormed out. She couldn't waste her energy on his peculiar reaction to her punishment. She shifted her thoughts back to their usual focus, escape.

* * *

Hours later, well into the night, Damian lay wide awake in his bed. Typically, he'd have been indulging in an assortment of sexual activities with several women of his choosing, an almost nightly ritual for him, but the slave witch still haunted his thoughts. Her deeply anguished gaze triggered something inside of him. Those shining blue eyes held some kind of significance.

Before he knew what he was doing, he was out of bed and pulling on his jeans. Shaking his head at his own ludicrous behavior, he downed a glass of whiskey from the bar in his bedchambers and headed for the door.

When Damian strode into the room, the witch was bent over at the foot of Raden's bed, tethered by a chain behind her neck that connected to her ankles, her wrists awkwardly bound behind her back.

Raden lowered the whip, eyeing Damian with concern. "What's happened?"

She had to be Raden's personal slave if he kept her in his chambers during the night. Fuck, this was not a good idea. But seeing the woman tied up in such a way while his uncle whipped her ignited a powerful reaction inside him. Damian used his mind's power to release her bonds. The chains fell away from her, and she crumpled to the floor.

"I want this slave."

Raden straightened. "She is mine."

"I want her."

"You are a weak little boy compared to me, nephew. She is loyal only to me, and since she happens to be a witch, your most dreaded adversary, this is a poor decision on your part." He snapped the whip at the floor beside her crouched body. "Sit up."

She obeyed him. Raden jerked the ethereal white collar around her throat before taking it off.

"Put Damian on his knees."

She kept her eyes downcast. With quivering hands, she centered her shimmering powers toward Damian. Her strange gold light snaked around his wrists.

He dropped to his knees under her will. *Fuck. This was a bad idea.*

"This one is much stronger than Marybelle. These golden powers will easily melt your flesh off the bone, and she is *mine* to control. Burn his face, slave." Raden shoved her forward. "Our future dark lord, maimed by a slave. No creature in Hell will follow a weak, deformed leader, Damian."

He kicked the girl, making her yelp. "I said burn him, witch!"

Shaking, she crawled forward, taking a closer look at Damian as she slowly reached for his face.

Damian stared at the floor with tightly clenched fists, fighting her firm restraints around his wrists. He'd already known this was a mistake. Now he was going to be mutilated for it.

Her palms brushed the shadow of facial hair along his jaw, and something sparked at the contact. Drawing closer to him, she pressed her hands to his skin. He read her thoughts, and they ran cold with fear. She didn't want to burn him, but Raden leered expectantly at her.

A vision raced through her mind, intimately huddled in Damian's arms. Images of herself running her glossy nails over his shortly buzzed hair, holding his face in her small hands.

Spurred by a strange longing, he turned his face into the witch's palm, drawn to her warmth.

"*Do it!*" Raden startled the witch out of her trance.

She jerked her hands back and cowered low on the floor. Raden raised his harsh whip. She trembled as her powers weakened, and the sparkling gold bonds disappeared.

Free from the fierce hold she had on him, Damian stood with a surge of adrenaline. He squared his shoulders and narrowed his eyes at Raden.

"I'm your future master, Uncle. She belongs to me now, is that clear?"

Raden flashed him a murderous look and tensed his jaw. He shifted his glare toward the witch, and she dropped her gaze. "It's clear." He pivoted toward the door. "I'll leave you with your new toy."

When the door slammed shut, Damian let out the breath he'd been holding. He had fucked up. He never should have taken on his uncle as an adversary, but something about this witch captivated him. He couldn't ignore the impulse to keep her close, regardless of the risk.

Damian picked up the magical collar and knelt beside her. "Lift up your hair."

CHAPTER FOUR

Haley wanted to cry at the gentle way her new master spoke such hateful words. She dismally pulled her long wavy curls off her neck as he clicked the collar closed around her throat.

He started for the door. "Follow me."

She stayed at his heel, crawling behind him as Raden had taught her.

Damian stopped. "No." He bent down and gestured for her to stand.

Haley rose on unsteady legs. Her beaten body hurt whenever she moved. She slowly struggled to walk beside him.

"I'm gonna carry you."

Haley flinched as his muscular arms lifted her off her feet. Shaking in his hold, she tried to relax her nerves as her new master brought her out of the evil mansion. Exhaustion took control of her body, and she fell in and out of sleep, vaguely aware she was airborne, surrounded by red sky. Raden's nephew still held her, though they seemed to be riding a winged creature of some kind. She wondered what new horrors awaited her as she drifted under.

***

She woke in a strange bed and sat up with a start. Candles lit the windowless room, lavishly furnished in dark, royal colors and, most importantly, empty. She was alone, at least for the moment, though the negative current in the air told her she was still in Hell. She reached for her neck and touched the wretched collar, still firmly attached. Memories of her new dark master flooded her mind. She pushed back the silk comforter and slid out of bed. Naked and dirty, deep cuts from the whip still covered her body, but the wounds had healed somewhat. How long had she been asleep?

She drifted toward a table full of delicious smelling food. Still hot. That fact sent a jolt of fear through her, but she chose to luxuriate in the moment. She spread butter onto a piece of steaming bread with a dull silver utensil and began to feel almost human again.

She walked into a large attached bathroom. A glass bottle sat beside the giant whirlpool bathtub. The distinctive blue liquid reminded her of a serum her brother, Stephen, sometimes used on open wounds when his healing powers weren't enough. The glass topper clinked when she took it off, and she dabbed it onto the split skin on her thigh. It closed instantly, changing into a nearly healed strip of pink.

She turned on the tub faucet and poured it into the water, turning it a dark shade of blue green.

After a long soak, her sore limbs began to revive. It was possible the new dark master allowed her to heal only to give her fresh wounds from his own hand.

To her amazement, there was a closet full of hanging clothes. Barely-there dresses and skirts and countless pairs of high heels in her exact size. She went through a chest of drawers full of lingerie, all of it sheer or strategically placed to show off her private areas. She chose a soft, thin nightgown and slid into the transparent fabric.

Gloriously clothed, she grabbed a bite of seasoned chicken breast from the hot tray before sliding back into bed.

* * *

Damian moved his hands behind his head, resting on the wide piece of cushioned furniture in the sitting room. The black ceiling in his mansion stretched several stories above him. The witch had been under his roof for three weeks, and as far as he knew, she hadn't left her room once, but as he stared up at the obsidian abyss, he was sure he could sense her intoxicating presence nearby.

His demon servants informed him she ate regularly and her wounds had healed. She didn't speak to them, fearful of them whenever they brought her food, and she was asleep more often than not.

"Master." The girl with her mouth on his halfway-stiff cock purred at him. She and the other woman at his testicles had been diligently working to arouse him for several minutes without any luck.

Damian couldn't keep his thoughts from wandering to the bewitching slave in his house. The strange vision he'd caught when she'd touched his face weeks earlier had plagued him. The effect she had on him was dangerous, he hadn't been able to achieve a full erection since he'd seen her.

He couldn't trust his servants alone with the witch, so he hadn't visited his home in Seattle since she'd arrived. He wanted to work on his car, the classic Chevelle he'd built from the ground up years earlier. It was due for an oil change and could use another tune-up, but the girl's safety was imperative, so he remained in Hell. Eventually he'd need to address her.

Haley peered down through the gaps in the black railing at the orgy below. The master was lying on his back, being sexually serviced by two naked women at his groin while two others kissed and groped each other across his torso. She backed away, shockingly repulsed, an unpleasant emotion bothering her stomach.

It was time to focus on escape once again. She went into a dim office. A silver dagger glimmered on the desk. After a few unsuccessful attempts to cut through the collar, she gave up.

"What you got there?"

Haley spun at the demon's voice and gripped the dagger as he stalked closer.

"Master has us waiting on a slave like you're one of the royal ones." He shook his reptilian head with a toothy grin. "No slave should be allowed to wear clothes. Drop the blade before I stick it in you, understand? You're coming with me to the dungeon."

She lowered the dagger to her side and obediently started forward.

The demon reached out to grab her. "No, no, bitch. Give me the blade."

Haley stretched it toward him with a jittering hand. "Here."

After weeks of rejuvenating sleep, her reflexes were back to normal. She thrust the dagger-point into his throat, and he hit the floor with a gurgling sound.

She grabbed a ring of keys from his pocket and ran toward the door.

A throng of demons waited in the hallway. Before she could cry out, one of them gagged her. A powerful fist smashed against the back of her head, sending cold chills down her spine, and she fell into a cloaking darkness.

She fluttered her eyes open as claws ran all over her naked skin. The monsters fondled her bare breasts, and Haley started screaming, working to free herself from their grasp.

"Make her be quiet!"

Another demon dangled his deformed penis over her face. "You're not gonna tell the master nothing. Or we'll shove a hot poker right up inside you."

They forced her legs apart. The demon above her jerked her mouth open for his oddly shaped organ, and she squeezed her eyes shut.

"Let her go. Master is coming!"

When Haley opened her eyes, black liquid oozed from gaping wounds in the demons' bodies. She sat upright as a blade sliced through one of their necks and the head tumbled to the ground.

Damian stood holding a dripping sword in the damp, dark cell. She turned away from his well-built naked body. He must have come straight from his orgy at the sound of her screams.

"Get her dressed and bring her to my chambers," he commanded the only living demon in the dungeon and headed out the door.

* * *

"Put this on." A wheezing demon threw a corset at her and rustled through the drawer in her room. He picked out a string thong for her to wear. "The master is finally gonna use you like the slave you are." He chuckled, uncomfortably close as she rapidly worked the dozen tiny hooks at her front to fasten the tight red lingerie. He held up the wad of black strings. "He told me to get you dressed. I'm gonna put this on you."

"I can do it." Haley reached for the little thong, and he growled.

"Master said." With deep concentration, he pushed the sheer fabric between her legs and wrenched the string up her backside.

"I'll do the rest." She worked to tear the strings from his grip, but he wouldn't have it.

"Master wants them up between these." The demon harshly yanked the fabric upward at her sex.

Haley tried to push him away, and her hand brushed the thick handle of a dagger hanging loosely from his breeches. Preoccupied, he stared plainly between her legs as he tied the strings with monstrous claws. She slid the blade free and moved it behind her back, tucking it under the corset, hidden by her long wave of thick loose curls.

Damian stood beside a wooden counter, pouring whiskey into a crystal tumbler when she slipped into his bedroom. He looked over the sheer red corset and tiny strip of black panties tied into bows at her hips.

Silent for a moment, he drank from his glass. "What's your name?"

Haley held her hands behind her back, poised to grab the knife, and struggled to keep her mind clear.

He set his drink down, moving closer until he stood in front of her, shirtless in jeans, hanging low without a belt. He clearly wasn't wearing underwear. Deep scars covered his muscled abdomen, possibly inflicted by the witch Raden had spoken of.

"Haley." Her voice came out as a weak whisper.

"Well, Haley." He paused, thoughtful for a moment. "I know your sole focus is escape, but I'm sorry to tell you that you're wasting your time."

"What else would I be doing with my time?"

Damian shrugged. "What do you like to do?"

She gripped her hands behind her, caught off guard by the question. "I know what you're doing."

He shoved his hands in his pockets and stared blankly at her.

"I saw your fantasy," she whispered. "When I touched you in your uncle's chambers. You want me to fall in love with you."

"That wasn't a fantasy." Damian's expression turned dark, and he filled his glass. "Look around, Haley. We're in Hell, there's no love here."

With his attention momentarily focused elsewhere, Haley withdrew the dagger. Rushing forward, she sank it into his heart and twisted.

Damian grabbed her wrists and swiftly forced her to the ground. "It'll require a lot more than that to take me down."

Crushed under his weight, Haley kneed him between his legs, and he grunted. She scrambled away from his loosened grasp.

He tackled her, then wrenched the dagger free from his chest and tossed it away. Gripping a handful of her hair, he pulled her to his bed.

"You fucking stabbed me."

She was a ball of energy, clawing at his arm. He picked her up and threw her onto the black silk sheets.

She hooked her nails into his neck, slicing through his skin, and tore free from him.

Damian caught his arm around her waist and pulled her backward. He slammed her onto the bed and held her down.

A sudden vision blinded her. Breathless, with Damian's face between her legs while sparkling golden lights floated through the air around her. He lapped at her with his tongue, and she clutched the sheets, sending magical golden sparkles from her fingers into the white fabric of a bed she'd never seen before.

He pressed his weight onto her. "Who's fantasizing now?"

"*You are.*" Surprisingly aroused, she struggled against him.

"I'm not. Stop moving." The softness beneath his rigid tone suggested he was also aroused.

"Then let me go." Haley freed her leg and brought it around his waist, writhing against his hardness.

"I said stop moving." He gripped her wrist before she could claw his face.

Another vision struck her. Damian, on his knees in the same unknown bed, lifted a dreamy Haley to straddle his lap. With his large cock inside her, she circled her arms around his neck, blissfully ascending from an earth-shattering orgasm.

He licked her naked breasts in the darkness. "You're so beautiful."

The vivid vision disappeared, and Damian loosened his hold on her wrist. "What the fuck was that?"

She jerked herself free, and he grasped her arms.

"Just…wait a minute." He wrestled her back under him.

"Let go." She leaned forward and snapped her teeth against his throat.

His hand flew to the back of her head, and he pulled a fistful of her hair backward. An image flashed in her mind of herself, naked except for a garter belt and black stockings. She bent over the hood of a glossy blue-and-white muscle car, and Damian plowed into her from behind, grunting low, pleasured groans.

"Stop showing me your fantasies!"

He pressed down on her with his smothering hold. "They're not my fucking fantasies."

She raked her hand up his slippery abdominal muscles to the bleeding wound in his chest and tried to shove her fingers inside.

Damian tightened his rough hold on her hair. "You little…fucking…"

Her eyes filled with tears at the sharp pain in her scalp. A shocking string of sensation flowed down to her sex, despite her boiling anger. Panting with effort, she twisted her hips against his enormous erection, restrained under his jeans. The tiny black panties rode up, straining against her clit. Her body responded, working her hips lower while the thin fabric stretched tighter.

Damian's eyes hooded at her sensual motions, and he yanked her wrists over her head, pinning them to the black leather headboard.

She rubbed herself against the front of his jeans. Squirming her knee between his legs, she slammed it into his groin.

His body clenched as he grunted in her ear. She broke free, flying off the bed.

He reached out and hooked his fingers into the strings at her hip. The delicate panties stretched against her sex before they snapped, loosely hanging off her hips. Adrenaline powered her toward the door, but Damian was faster. He swept her feet out from under her, and she fell forward onto the black marble floor. She had more fight left in her. For the first time in months, she was well-fed and fully rested. She would not give in to punishment so quickly.

CHAPTER FIVE

Damian hauled her up, preparing to toss her back onto the sheets, but she clawed at his jeans. Jerking open the top button, she grasped his zipper. He wasn't about to let her anywhere near his dick and worked to keep his hold on her while pushing her hands away.

Haley shoved her hand down the front of his halfway open jeans, bypassing his firm cock, and tightened her fingers around his testicles, squeezing them mercilessly in her palm. Every muscle in his torso clenched at the shocking pain as he bent forward.

"Please let go." He held her forearm with strained hands.

"Not until you let me go." She unzipped his jeans for a better grasp, freeing his erect cock from his open zipper.

Damian groaned. "I can't just let you go."

"Yes, you can! Please let me go home."

He roughly grabbed her shoulders, pushing her to the floor, and she took him down with her.

She pulled him forward by his bruised testicles.

The renewed stab of pain sent a fire of anger through him, and he reached down and pried her fingers away from his tender flesh.

Haley gave him a begging look. "Please, I just want you to let me go."

"That will never happen." Growling, finally loose from her desperate clutch, he wrenched her toward him by her wrists. Tears streamed down her face as he pulled her back to his bed, her bare skin sliding along the marble. "I have *lost* my patience with you. You're lucky I don't cane you for this, fucking little troublemaker." He threw her down to the black sheets. They were drenched in his blood.

Haley stared at the door, and he snapped his fingers in front of her face.

"Run if you want. I'll drag you back to this bed all night if I have to."

She looked pitiful, her blue eyes teary and beaten with fatigue. Blood soaked the sheer corset, her panties torn halfway off, leaving her lower half exposed.

Bolting past him, she sprinted for the door. He caught her in a powerful hold and walked her backward. She struggled in his grasp.

He leaned into her ear. "What do you think is on the other side of that door? It's guarded by demons."

"Then I'll kill them like I killed the others." Haley caught his gaze. "After I kill you."

A vision struck his thoughts. He held her cold body over his lap, looking down at her dead face, and a crushing emotion made his chest tense up. The sharp agony subsided as the vision faded, leaving only the burning pain of the stab wound.

"What are you doing to me?" He pushed her down onto the bed. "Beautiful little witch. You're trying to torment me. What are those visions? Something you've imagined? How do you know what my car looks like?"

"Those sex visions are obviously *your* imagination. I'm the one you're holding captive, why would I fantasize about you, arrogant...rapist...prick." Her eyes seemed to catch fire as she spoke, and she thrashed his face and chest with her nails.

He yanked her closer, binding her arms in a tight embrace. "I'm not a rapist. I just rescued you from being raped, for fuck's sake." He covered her fighting body with all of his weight. "Tell me about the visions."

"I can't breathe." Haley sobbed against his bloodied chest.

"Then answer quickly."

"I don't know what they are! They're the first ones I've had with the collar on. I can't breathe. Please, Damian…"

He jerked back with a sudden breath. It was the first time she'd called him by name, and the sound set something off in him.

Panting beneath him, Haley looked up into his eyes.

"Let me assure you, I'm not a rapist. But you're sleeping in here tonight. In my bed. I should tie you up," he grabbed a handful of her hair, pulling at the base of her neck, "but I'd rather just hold onto this all night."

She shook her head. "I will stab you in your sleep, I promise."

His naked cock lay between them, the hardness mashed against her stomach, and she tried to wriggle away from him. Leery of her movements, Damian leaned in closer.

"I swear to Christ, if you kick me in the balls one more time, I'm gonna have to tie you down."

She parted her legs and wrapped her thighs around him. Her hips tilted toward him as she squirmed closer.

He growled at the friction of his still swollen testicles against her soft private area.

"Succubus. I'm not falling for it."

"I would never, *ever* have sex with you," she whispered.

"That's not what your pussy is telling me, Haley. You're all kinds of wet down there." He dragged his erection lower and hovered his mouth over hers. "I wouldn't fuck you if you begged me."

"Don't even suggest it." She slid her gaze away from him. "I don't want you either."

"Please. Your thighs are so tight around me right now. You want it."

Her lower lip trembled.

"I saw your fantasy. I know you want me to lick you."

"That wasn't my fantasy."

He slipped his length along her wet slit. "I don't know, Haley. Your thoughts are pretty focused on my cock right now. And I do have this nagging urge to find out how you taste."

"You're repulsive." She breathed the words.

"You imagined me holding you in the dark, telling you how beautiful you are."

"*You* imagined those things…" She pulled her brows together with a tiny shake of her head.

"When was the last time you came, Haley?"

57

"What?" Her breath quickened. "I don't have to answer tha—"

"Just tell me. When did you last have an orgasm?"

"I don't know." She looked away. "I don't remember."

"I want to make you come."

Her gaze flashed toward his. She opened her mouth to respond, but he buried her words under his kiss, slowly tasting her.

"This is what I can do to your pussy if you let me." His words resounded inside her head as he stroked his tongue along hers. *"Say yes to me."*

Her thoughts dreamily agreed to whatever he asked.

Damian stopped kissing her and moved lower. He let his tongue glide over her clitoris and almost moaned at her intoxicating taste.

Gasping, Haley shoved his shoulders, but he didn't move from between her thighs. He needed more. He brushed his lips across her supple pussy.

She let out a shaky breath. "No one's ever…kissed me there before."

Damian groaned against her soft flesh. His cock was ready to explode at the pressure coursing through it.

He trailed his tongue along her slit, savoring the taste. He'd never enjoyed oral sex, but there was a strange familiarity to the insatiable desire.

He morphed to his forked, demonic tongue and gave it to her freely, sliding it through her pussy, then flicked his magical tongue across her clit over and over, teasing her until she was trembling beneath him. He'd never wanted so badly to hear a woman come.

Her nails skidded over the back of his head, and she moved her sweet pussy closer to his mouth. He scraped his teeth over her plump clit, and it pulsed under his tongue.

Softly moaning his name, she held him firmly against her gushing orgasm.

He licked her thoroughly, aching between his legs, then trailed his forked tongue upward. Her stomach quivered under his lips as he tasted along the scarred skin.

He slowly unhooked the front of her corset. He wanted to hear her make that sound again.

"Don't touch my stomach." She turned her face, hiding behind her palms.

He kept unhooking her strapless corset, disturbed by the affectionate emotions moving through his chest. "Why not?" He loosened the last hook, and the red fabric fell open, freeing her heavy breasts. He ran his palm between them, bringing his fingertips down her body, and brushed across the large R branded to the side of her belly button.

"It hurts," she whimpered behind her hands.

Though it was still new, the burn had healed. She was insecure about the scar?

Lowering his head, he brought his mouth to her throat, and visible chills broke out along her skin. "You know you're beautiful, witch. Don't pretend you aren't seducing me right now. Even with the collar on, I'm powerless to you."

Haley refused to look at him, and he knew he was breaking her down. "Why do I want you so much? I shouldn't want you."

"Because my cock can make you feel good," he breathed into her ear. "You deserve to feel good, Haley." He touched her bare breasts, holding them in his hands. "I want to hear what it sounds like when you come on my cock. You make the sexiest sounds when you come."

"I thought you wouldn't fuck me if I begged you."

"Let me fuck you." He could hardly breathe at the thought of it.

She slid away from him to the other side of his bed.

He kept silent for a moment. Frustrated, he debated whether to just leave her alone for the night. He'd never had to pursue anyone for sex before, women had always been readily available for him. He wasn't accustomed to rejection, but it only made him want her more.

"You didn't like the way my tongue felt?"

Haley glanced over at him. "I liked it."

He moved toward her, and she leaned away from his touch.

"If you don't want my cock, maybe you'll let me slide my tongue inside you." He'd do anything to get another taste.

"No."

Damian paused. Her thoughts brimmed with sensual desire, and his cock grew painfully hard at her arousal. "I already know what you want, just say it."

"Why don't you just *take it*? I'm your captive, remember? Why are you pretending to be morally upright?"

"I'm not a rapist."

"Well, that is a rare quality around here."

The stab of pain in her voice triggered an intense protective instinct inside him.

He pushed his erection down into his jeans and zipped them. Taking her arm, he drew her closer. "I know they raped you. My uncle and his demons."

Haley leaned into him. She nodded under his chin.

"I'm not gonna let anyone hurt you again."

"I don't believe you." She nuzzled closer. "You can't keep me here forever."

"I'll keep you as long as I like." He plunged his fingers into her thick cinnamon hair. "Lie down with me. Let's go to sleep."

The wound in his chest was still bleeding, and he felt slightly off from all the blood loss. He pulled her against him as he sank into a plush black pillow. She relaxed in his hold.

The intimate position seemed strangely routine as he drifted asleep.

***

Startled awake, consumed by a deep shock of emptiness, he shot up in bed. The haunting vision of the seductive witch, lying dead in his arms had plagued his dreams.

The sight of her sleeping serenely beside him set off more unwelcome emotions he'd never felt before.

He climbed out of bed, ignoring the unsettling tenderness in his chest. Her taste still lingered on his lips, and he poured a glass of whiskey to calm his nerves. She was changing things somehow, and he had a lot at stake.

His focus should be on the new station he was about to take as leader of Hell, not the slave in his chambers.

CHAPTER SIX

Haley roused from heavy sleep to find Damian naked across the room, pulling on a pair of gray sweatpants. The wounds she'd inflicted on him had practically healed.

"I've had your clothes moved to another room." He tossed a black silk robe onto the bed.

She slid it on with a frown. He meant to put her in the dungeon. Lowering her gaze, she slowly moved off his bed and followed him out the door.

He stopped at a guest room nearby and the tension in her body loosened.

"Meet me in the dining room for breakfast." Without looking at her, he turned and continued down the hall.

She took a shower in the new bathroom and cleaned his blood off her body with shaking hands. His cold tone frightened her. She thought of all the serial killers that wined and dined prostitutes before brutally murdering them.

He seemed more pliable when she was underdressed, so she selected a black corset that covered her ugly scar and tiny panties that were just thin ribbons laced over her sex. Then she slipped on a pair of black high heels.

Keeping her thoughts clear, she wandered past the empty kitchen and snagged a large knife from a magnetic strip on the wall. She slid it up her back, hiding it under her corset.

In the dining room, Damian was standing beside the long table, chewing a piece of bacon when he saw her and forced his gaze away. "What are you wearing?"

She shrugged a shoulder. "Practically nothing."

"I can see that," he grumbled.

Haley ate a few grapes from the table and drifted closer to him. "Does it bother you?"

"You can wear whatever you like."

She moved her fingers under the dainty ribbons across her pussy, drawing his gaze to her hand as she teased herself. She used the other to pull his waistband down and stroked her palm along his growing cock.

In a swift motion, she grasped the knife at her back and held the edge of the blade to his groin. "Take off my collar."

His eyes turned black as he took hold of her wrist with a jerking grip, and her fingers loosened around the knife's handle.

"You think I haven't had those cut off before?" He stepped forward, startling her. "Being immortal makes me an interesting torture subject." He held her wrist with a steel grip until she let go of the weapon, and the blade clattered to the floor. "*Bad* girl."

Damian pulled out a high-backed chair from the side of the dining table and laid her over his lap as he sat down. He wrenched her panties down her legs and spanked her bare backside, slapping it hard. She could feel his hard naked cock pressed against her stomach.

Her pussy surged with sensation at the abrupt smacks from his open palm. She swallowed the aroused moan in her throat.

Damian stood her up, and she stumbled a little in her high heels, holding her hands against her sore backside, staring at him as heat flooded her face.

Rising from his chair, he put away his raging erection, covering it in his sweatpants, and eyed her panties, still gathered down around her knees. He shifted his glare away from her.

She promptly brought the ribbons up around her hips, shaken and flushed with arousal.

"I know you want your freedom." He ran his palm over his mouth and shook his head. "Very soon, I'll take over the throne and replace my father as the dark lord. Raden is already upset that I took you. If he found out I also freed you, he'd lead an uprising against me. The ascension rituals have already begun. As soon as I finish them and receive the dark power, I will reign over Hell." He glanced at her with stunningly beautiful green eyes. "If you can remain passive until then, I'll give you your freedom."

Still unnerved by the longing sensation in her sex, she stood silent for a moment. "Why would you do that?"

"I don't need a slave, especially one as cumbersome as you. I have more pressing things to concern myself with."

She couldn't bring herself to trust him. "So, you'll just release me when you come into power."

"As long as you're compliant, I'll send you wherever you'd like to go."

"I don't believe you."

Damian shrugged. "You'll have to trust me."

Haley pressed her lips together. "False hope is the worst kind of torture," she whispered. "I won't be obedient until you take off my collar."

"Absolutely not."

"I won't hurt you." Haley took a step toward him. "Without the collar, I could read your mind and know for sure what your intentions are."

"My thoughts are guarded, you couldn't read them anyway, and if I took off your collar, I'd be at your mercy. That's never gonna happen." He gave her a dark stare. "When I receive the powers of the throne, and I'm stronger than your magic, that's when the collar comes off."

"You have to give me something." She gripped her hands together. "I can't just give up the fight because you made a promise. It'll be a demonstration of mutual trust."

Damian remained silent, and she continued.

"It isn't just about my powers. The collar is…degrading. It makes me feel weak and chained, like a pet. I promise I won't ever hurt you again. Read my mind, you'll see that I'm telling the truth."

"I was reading your mind when you stabbed me, and when you attempted to castrate me. You apparently have a way of hiding your thoughts."

"Then look harder." Her lower belly clenched as arousal ran through her, and she caught her bottom lip between her teeth.

Damian hesitated for a moment, then entered her mind and started poring through her thoughts and memories. Emotion welled in her chest as he caught glimpses of her happy life before her capture, surrounded by smiling faces. Now, she focused all her energy and life force on one goal: freedom. There were no malicious thoughts toward him.

"I can see you liked that spanking a little more than you let on."

She swallowed, her backside still stinging from his abrupt punishment. Her heart pounded as he reached toward her and grasped the collar. The powerful restraint snapped open, and he set it on the table.

Haley touched her bare neck, overwhelmed by the small victory. "Are you really gonna let me go?" She tried to stifle the hopeful joy rising inside her.

"If you can keep yourself from knifing me until then." He looked at her scantily clad body. "I don't know where you keep pulling those out from."

"I promise I'll be good." Haley felt a hint of a smile forming on her lips for the first time since she'd been abducted.

"Better be, or I'll have to spank you again." He reached for a piece of fruit, and Haley gingerly took hold of his arm. He flinched slightly at her touch.

Her mind reading powers came to life, opening his inner thoughts to her, revealing a string of bone-chilling torture imagery. Damian, strapped to a table. A tiny witch with short black hair cooing at him in a sing-song voice. Her hands painfully toying with him. She called him her pet while she burned and tormented his naked body with her black powers.

Flooded with warm tenderness for him, Haley moved closer, and he stiffened at her power-charged touch. She slipped her arms up around his neck and pressed her forehead against his throat. "Thank you."

"Mmhm." Damian stood stone-still in her embrace. He cleared his throat. "I'll take the throne in a matter of days. We're going to the palace today for another ritual."

"We?" She peeked up from under his chin.

"Yes, you're coming with me. Consider changing your clothes."

Haley nodded. Her hug was obviously making him uncomfortable. She let go of him and backed away. Exuberantly free without the dreadful collar, she picked up a plump strawberry from the table. Something inside wouldn't let her get too excited about the possibility of Damian keeping his word, but she had her powers back. Her hand rested loosely at the base of her neck as she dipped the fruit into some delectable cream sauce and took a bite.

"Is your father going to be there?" Her stomach twisted at the idea of coming face to face with Satan.

"Possibly. Not likely though, he hasn't been present for any of the rituals so far." Damian took the chair he'd used to put her over his knee and pushed it back toward the side of the lengthy table. He sat down in front of a plate of eggs.

A ripple of sensation returned to her sex in remembrance of his spanking. She slid onto the table, sitting just next to his plate, and continued eating her strawberry. Damian kept his eyes on his plate as she crossed her legs.

"Is your father as nice as you are?"

He snorted and picked up a crystal goblet. "You think I'm nice? I just spanked you."

A smile spread across her lips, and she reached backward for a handful of grapes. "I sort of had it coming."

Damian pushed his plate to the side, looking at her intently. He took hold of her hips and shifted her over until she was in front of him.

Her gaze sharpened. Chewing on her grape, she reluctantly let her crossed ankles rest on the side of his leg.

"You liked it." He uncrossed her bare legs, moving her black patent heel across his lap. She kept her knees close together, though both heels rested at either side of him.

"I didn't." Haley swallowed, turning away from his searing gaze, and set the rest of her grapes on a stray plate.

"Don't lie to me. I saw your thoughts."

"Why would I like that?" Her breathing slowed as his hands went to her knees.

"Probably because you knew you were a naughty girl and needed a spanking." He slowly spread her legs apart. "You did try to cut off my balls."

"I wasn't gonna actually do it," she whispered, staring down into his luminous eyes as he opened her legs wider.

"You wore this to distract me?" He slid his hand up her inner thigh, and she grew wet with anticipation.

"Mmhm."

"But not so I would tear it off you."

Her breath caught, and she shook her head.

"So you're a tease."

Haley forced a deep breath, betrayed by her hips, moving forward in want of his touch. He hooked his fingers into her wet panties, jerking her toward him, and she sat at the edge of the table, her legs spread wide.

His masculine knuckles brushed against her heated pussy. "Answer me."

"Yes." She stared at him with a hooded gaze. "I'm a tease."

"I think I'll punish you for being such a little cock-tease."

Her pulse shot up. "No…"

"Lie back on the table." His voice went cold, and Haley couldn't breathe in the tight corset, frozen.

"You said you'd obey me, witch." He softened his tone, though it still sounded deadly. "Are you going back on your word?"

"No." Shaking, she did as he commanded, leaning backward until her back touched the wooden table.

"Good girl." He stood up between her thighs and let go of her underwear, continuing in a raw voice. "Show me your pussy."

Her teeth sank into her bottom lip, chills spreading over her skin as she tugged her panties to the side and widened her legs. She could feel his intense gaze on her bare sex.

"Open it for me."

Her cheeks ran hot as she pulled her tender lips apart, showing him the slick moisture on her clitoris. It thudded with hunger in her painfully exposed position, heatedly craving any stimulation.

Damian took her wrists and stretched her arms over her head. "I like your hands up here. Don't move them, understand?" She nodded, clutching her hands into fists as she struggled to keep them in place above her.

With demanding fingers, he pulled open the ribbon closures along the front of her black corset, tearing the straps apart at her shoulders and slid it out from under her. Her nipples hardened instantly at their exposure. He rudely stripped away her skimpy panties, ripping the flimsy fabric from her open legs. Haley curled her fingers over the edge of the table above her, her face burning as she displayed her naked body for him.

Her heavy breathing was the only sound in the room. Damian dipped his fingers into the bowl of sweet cream on the table and spread it onto her taut nipples. She gasped at the cold sensation. He ran his fingers over her pussy, and the chilled cream trickled down her flesh.

Haley pursed her lips when he started to suck on her breast. She craved his mouth at the dripping cream between her legs, almost lifting her hips off the table with need.

His rough mouth left her nipple plump and sore, and he gently grasped her hurting breast, mindlessly holding it while he picked up a spear of cantaloupe. Damian watched her face as he slowly inserted it inside her, working it in and out of her, and dragged the tip of it upward, running it over her clit, covered in the syrupy cream. He took a bite of the melon before sitting down in the chair.

Haley couldn't hold in her cry when his tongue raked over her. He seemed motivated by her outburst, shoving the bitten melon back inside of her, and feasted on the sugary coating over her sex, licking her deeply.

"Oh, please. Please…" Her thoughts cried out to him as he licked her clean. She almost shrieked when he pulled his mouth away, leaving her writhing.

Damian pulled the cantaloupe out of her and put it in his mouth, chewing it while he stood. He squeezed an orange slice over her stomach, dripping the juice along her skin and onto her needy pussy. Her toes curled in her shoes, and she gripped the table in desperation as Damian kissed and sucked at her stomach, lapping up the juice. She trembled under him, shrinking into the table as his tongue dragged over her scarred skin, sending a shiver of revulsion through her, and her hand fell to her side to cover herself.

He caught her wrist and pressed it firmly to the table just over her head. His mouth went to her other breast. He sucked on her candied nipple, devouring the vulnerable pink flesh, and the sensation flowed down to her achingly neglected clit.

Damian tasted along the plump side of her breast and let his greedy tongue wander all over her exposed body. She sighed when his hot mouth closed over her pussy, panting softly as he brought her closer and closer, licking up every last drop of juice from her clit. When he had thoroughly cleaned every part of her with his tongue, Damian abruptly stood.

He pulled her upright on the table, and Haley shuddered. *He can't leave me like this.*

"We're leaving in a few minutes, go get dressed."

She forced herself to keep from flashing him a needy look, refusing to look at him at all. Her thoughts raged at him, he'd brought her so close only to deny her the divine release she craved so deeply. *He's punishing me.* What a horribly awful, wonderful punishment.

She didn't want to give him the satisfaction of knowing how strongly he'd affected her. Brimming with jittering pangs of arousal, she hopped down from the table and worked to hide her thoughts from him as she wordlessly slipped out of the dining room.

Dreadfully naked, wearing only a pair of high heels, Haley rushed through the mansion halls. She desperately wanted to massage herself with her fingers, to finish what Damian had so cruelly left unfinished, but decided against it. She only had a few minutes and didn't want him to catch her in the act.

She pulled on a tight black dress, the most modest of her options. Though it was strapless, the skirt was fuller than the rest, padded by layers of black tulle underneath. The form-fitting bodice was almost suffocating, trussing up her large breasts, exposing more cleavage than she would have liked, but it would have to do.

Damian knocked on the door as she struggled with the zipper, breathing heavily with her hands behind her back, tightly grasping the dainty closure. She could see him in her head, standing outside the door, fully dressed now in jeans and a collared shirt, the sleeves rolled to his elbows. With her powers back in full force, she could sense his energy in her thoughts and successfully closed him out of her head.

Her victory didn't last. He bypassed her mental blockades and spoke directly into her mind. *"Finish yourself off quickly, Haley, it's time to leave."*

High-strung, gripped with sexual frustration, she gasped and pulled open the rich wooden door. "Finish?"

CHAPTER SEVEN

Damian looked down at her black satin dress, loosely holding in her half-exposed breasts while she held it closed with one hand at her back. He'd heard her panting breaths on the other side of the door and pictured her touching herself. His assumption was all but confirmed when she'd promptly pushed him out of her thoughts. "Do you need help?"

Haley took a heavy breath. "Yes, please."

Damian moved around to her back. He ran his thumb along her bare skin before pulling up the zipper so that the dress was tightly snug around her middle. It billowed out into a bouncy skirt that stopped just below her backside, and he fought the urge to lift it and see what kind of panties she was wearing.

"Ready?" he muttered, still studying the bottom of her skirt from behind, his cock lengthening at the sight of her shapely legs and black high heels.

"Yes."

He slid his fingers around her elbow, moving beside her to lead her to the door.

Haley stopped. "Wait, I forgot…"

She swept past him and hurried to the armoire against the wall. She snatched a bundle of transparent black lace from a drawer, then carefully stepped her stilettos through it and pulled the panties up her thighs. They dipped low in the back, leaving her firm backside only halfway covered with sheer lace, and tied into a ribbon bow above the sexy cutout. Damian sat down on the bed, staring at her as she held up her skirt in the back, working to properly tie the bow.

Haley glanced over at him. "Can you help me, please?"

He dragged his hand along his rugged jawline, eyeing her with his head tilted to the side, and stood up. Haley let the black ribbons fall freely, holding her dress high above her hips. Damian stood behind her, his cock pumping with rolling desire as he gently took hold of the flimsy ribbons and tied them together just under the dimples on her lower back. The bow hung over her practically bare ass, and his palm itched to grasp it firmly.

Clenching his hand into a tight fist, Damian turned for the hallway without a word. He wouldn't be able to make it through the day without spanking her again, not after seeing what was underneath her dress. She was almost begging him for it anyway.

Haley followed close behind him out to the hall. Her heels clicked softly on the marble as they walked through the foyer.

He opened the massive black door at the mansion's entrance and ushered her outside. His dragon rested on the charcoal ground nearby and came to attention upon seeing him approach.

Haley fixed her wide-eyed gaze on the mighty reptile, and Damian continued guiding her toward the dragon with his hand against her lower back.

Her steps slowed the closer they got, and the dragon seemed to notice her agitation, its pupils dilating as it licked its forked tongue over its snout. Damian slid his palm around hers, gently tugging her along.

"You've ridden him before."

With a tiny nod, she let him pull her forward.

He climbed onto the dragon's back and lifted her up so that she faced him. He watched her, catching a glint of fear in her eyes as she brought her leg over the neck, and pulled her closer, holding her tight against his chest. As the beast gained speed, she rested against him, closing her eyes. Black clouds swirled in the red sky around them.

"Did you touch yourself?"

She looked up at him with a stern expression. "No."

"Good. I don't want you to. In fact, you're not allowed to."

Haley raised her eyebrows. Her thoughts raged with the urge to reach under her skirt and willfully disobey him right in the middle of the sky. "Why not?"

He tried to hide his smirk. "I'm the only one allowed to touch your pussy today."

"But you didn't let me come…"

"That's because you were being a little cock-tease. I needed to punish you."

"Punish me all you like. Your cock will remain untouched." Her cheeks blushed scarlet red. "I like being a cock-tease."

He seethed out a breath. "You're gonna regret saying that."

Haley chewed on her bottom lip for a moment, then held her cheek against his chest, drifting her arms around him.

Her delicate embrace provoked an onslaught of shocking vulnerable emotions, and he released his hold on her. He suddenly wished he'd given in to her pleas and just set her free instead of prolonging his time with her. Whatever retaliation Raden had in store for him had to be less terrifying than this strange, consuming intimacy with the witch.

When the dragon landed, she looked up at the grand entrance to the palace made of dark stone and looming towers. It was impossible to take in the ominous structure all at once, and she stared in awe.

Damian jumped down onto the hard black gravel, then took hold of her waist and helped her to the ground. Holding tightly to his bicep, she moved with reluctance on the way to the ornately detailed iron door. A seven-foot-tall demon guarded the door, extra limbs protruding from its torso, clad in black armor.

"Welcome home, Master." The monster pulled open the heavy door.

They walked into a wide hall that stretched on beyond comprehension, the transparent glass ceiling at least a hundred feet above them. The red sky illuminated the black floor, the moving clouds above leaving it dark in places.

"This is your home?" Her voice was barely a whisper, breaking the silence of the empty space. Her fingertips bit into his arm as they walked deeper into the palace, surrounded on either side by floor-to-ceiling murals depicting devilish creatures eating each other and bloody torture scenes.

"This is where I grew up."

Haley glanced away from the giant demonic statues. "You were a...child once?"

"Yeah."

"Here?" She sounded mortified.

"Master." A scratchy voice spoke up behind them, and he turned as a hobbling creature shuffled toward them. "The high priests are ready for you in the dining hall, breakfast is waiting."

"I already had breakfast, I'll meet with them after, and we can begin the ritual."

"Excellent, Master. A pleasure to serve you." The demon bowed his head as he retreated.

Damian kept walking down the hall, and the giant space curved slightly, branching off into multiple pathways. He pulled her toward a stairway made of black stone, and she kept her gaze trained downward as they passed between the two demons guarding the bottom of the stairs.

"Master." They regarded him with bowed heads as he ascended the staircase.

She clutched his arm as they moved down a smaller hall lined with several doorways. He stopped at the door with a twisted iron handle.

Haley loosened her hold on him as she stepped into the large room, lit by burning black candles on either side of his bed. Snarling faces were carved into the headboard of the ancient bedframe, looking down on the black silken bedding. His red Les Paul guitar leaned against the wall, the only stab of color in his gloomy bedroom.

She jumped at the sound of the creaking door latch, and he dropped the iron lock securely into place. She straightened as he brushed past her on the way to his desk at the corner of the room.

"My cock will remain untouched." He grasped the heavy chair from behind the gnarled desk and easily swiveled it to the middle of the dark chamber. "Is that what you said?"

Haley wrapped her arms around herself as he took a seat in the chair.

"Well." He eyed her, and she swallowed.

"Yes."

He studied her hourglass shape. "That deserves a spanking, Haley."

Her eyes glittered at him, and she clutched her arms across her waist.

His cock was thudding with desire as he beckoned her with his finger, and let it fall back to his lap. He shifted in his chair to better accommodate the bulging organ in his jeans.

Her knees trembling, she stood in place for a few moments, then slid her gaze away as she took a step forward and slowly approached him.

She delicately bent across his lap, and he lifted the folds of black fabric, pulling back the satin and tulle until her lacy panties came into view.

He fingered the little black bow he'd tied himself and glided his palm over the lovely mixture of transparent lace and supple skin. Her legs dangled at his side, and she opened her thighs a little over his lap. He couldn't help but slide his hand into the cutout in her panties, bringing his fingers down to her pussy, wet with arousal. As he rubbed his rough fingertips along her clit, her limbs melted over his legs, and she spread her knees farther apart for him.

While his fingers massaged her warm pussy, he circled her tender little spot of flesh with the pad of his thumb.

Sudden flashbacks of Raden's chambers filled her thoughts as she remembered squeezing her eyes shut, sending her mind to another place while Raden had violated her anally.

At the sight of his uncle in her mind, Damian immediately took his thumb away, his lust replaced with murderous anger. He contemplated the repercussions of executing his own uncle after taking the throne.

He wanted to make her forget the memories, rubbing her clit deeply, and swirled his thumb around her opening instead. His fingers found their way inside her, and she moaned quietly at the floor, *"Oh, please. Please don't stop touching me…"*

As he sank his fingers into her tight flesh, he groaned in frustration. God, he wished it was his cock. Her tempting little body lay over his painful erection, and he hadn't come at all since he'd first laid eyes on her. His balls were agonizingly sore from lack of release, not to mention her rough treatment of them, and the teasing games she played with him.

Her hips responded to his attention, moving against his hand as she writhed in his lap. He'd had enough, his cock was in too much pain. He slid his hand away from her drenched sex and out of her dainty panties. Haley cried out.

"I'm so close…"

"This is still a punishment, sexy witch. Are you ready for your spanking?"

Her heels swung loosely over his lap as she helplessly hung her head, and her long wavy locks brushed along the floor. "Yes."

His cock surged with need at her anguished answer. He pulled apart the ribbons he'd tied and ripped her pretty underwear off her, tearing away the thin fabric. His open hand came down hard onto her bare backside.

He spanked her again and again, bringing her fair skin to a ripe pink color. His cock was ready to burst behind the constraints of his zipper.

Haley spread her legs under his heavy hand. He couldn't resist and slapped her right on the moist mound of plump flesh. She made a startled sound but opened her legs wider, and he smacked her soft pussy again. He almost growled with desire when she raised her hips, allowing him better access to her sex.

Tension mounted between her legs. Somehow thrilled by her nakedness, Haley arched her back, pressing into his erection against her stomach as she tilted her clitoris toward his abrupt hand.

She moaned as he moved his large palm over her heated chest and into the front of her dress. He groped her breasts with one hand while he spanked her with the other, the tips of his fingers hitting her sensitive clit with every slap. Her nipples stiffened, sore from the rough way he'd mouthed them at breakfast, and she moaned at his roaming fingers under her tight dress.

Her skin was hot from his stinging slaps, and he slowed his hand, massaging and stroking the burning skin. Haley wrapped her fingers around his forearm as he fondled her breast and turned her face toward it, pressing her cheek against his tattooed muscle. She brought her lips to his scars, softly kissing them, and his body tensed beneath her.

Damian lifted her up, swiveling her hips so she sat sideways on his lap, her high heels dangling just above the floor, and her arms fell around him. She hid her face against his neck, barely able to sit still. Her backside hurt from his forceful spanking, and his skilled hands had only stoked the burning hunger between her legs. *When will he give me release?* She clutched tightly to his broad shoulders.

His thoughts were surprisingly open to her once again, though he'd mentioned before they were guarded.

Strange that she could read his mind when no one else could. His mind swarmed with a wild torrent of fragmented feelings, panicked by the tender way she touched him. It seemed he didn't want her around him anymore.

She quickly retreated from his mind, her heart somehow pained, and tried to regain a semblance of composure. Releasing her desperate hold on his large frame, she stood up from his lap, almost tumbling to the floor as she found her footing in the high heels.

Suddenly the ache in her sex didn't seem as pressing. The gnawing disappointment of being unwanted by Damian set into her stomach. Why did it hurt? Even if he did somehow want something more from her, she could never be with him. He was the future dark lord of Hell, for God's sake.

She smoothed out her skirt, uncomfortably naked under the short dress, and ran her fingers through the tangles in her hair. It wasn't just the way her body reacted to him, her spirit seemed affected as well, drawn to him in some way far beyond simple gratitude.

"I have a ritual to complete," Damian said in a hollow voice.

He stood and moved the chair back in front of the desk, then walked swiftly past her. She folded her arms across herself, somber as he unbolted the door without another word to her.

She swallowed the lump of emotion in her throat and followed him out into the hallway. Soon she would be back in Seattle, and he'd be nothing more than a distant memory.

CHAPTER EIGHT

"Hey, little brother, who's this?"

The deep voice belonged to a robust man approaching them in the hall, regarding Haley with dark eyes. His long black hair swung loosely at his wide shoulders, his arms and neck coated in black tattoos. His name resounded through her thoughts as her psychic powers came to life. Karver. Damian had a brother?

"So you're the famous slave girl Uncle Raden's been screaming about to anyone who'll listen." He stood directly in her pathway, giving her a lewd onceover.

She let out a tiny cry as Damian grabbed her waist, bringing her to his side, and kept moving. She struggled to keep up with his rushed pace, her heels tapping quickly against the floor.

Karver easily held Damian's determined stride, and two other men, built of pure muscle, appeared from around a corner, joining them in the hall. They had the same dark features, likely more of Damian's brothers.

"Where are you running off to? About to get nasty with your stolen slave girl?" One of the towering men stepped in front of Damian, blocking his path.

Damian halted, his fingers digging into her side. "Move, Mordecai."

"We just want to have a little fun with your new plaything. She's not technically yours, Damian." Karver tilted his head with a smirk.

"You think you can take all three of us?" Mordecai laughed. "Remember when you were younger and we'd all take turns holding you down and just beat the living shit out of you?"

"He thinks now that everyone calls him Master, he's better than us."

"Onyx is right, Damian." Mordecai continued. "You pulled rank on our own uncle. And after he saved you from that little witch's torture table! You need to learn a lesson in humility. We're taking your slave girl."

"You're not gonna touch her."

"We're all immortal here, Damian, except for your little toy. You're laughably outnumbered. Just give her over." Karver crowded closer, leaning into his face.

Mordecai grinned in Haley's direction, and she shuddered. "I'm gonna knife your ugly twat, girl."

Damian slipped a blade from his pocket and sliced open Karver's throat. He grabbed a stunned Mordecai by the collar and stabbed the knife into his mouth, bringing forth a chilling scream, gurgled with blood.

Haley's eyes widened in horror as a piece of the man's tongue fell in a crimson wave down his chin.

Karver fell to his knees, holding his gaping neck as blood poured out of the open wound.

"Onyx." Damian looked to the silent third man whose eyes had gone black with hatred. "Do you want to lose any body parts?"

His brother shook his head and turned in another direction.

Haley stared at the wounded men as they choked on their own blood, and Damian took her arm, leading her away from the macabre scene. They rushed down the staircase, and she lost her footing on the steps. He caught her just before she landed on her sore backside, pulling her upright, and slowed his pace a bit.

Still in shock, the edges of her vision blurred as they headed down a massive hall. A faint sound of chanting echoed somewhere nearby.

She gasped as Damian pulled her to the side of the hall. He ducked into a small passageway that stretched on into darkness.

He drew her deeper into the shadows and halted. Turning to her, he pressed her back against the stone wall, then took her face into his hands, and his soft lips crashed into hers.

Her body vibrated at the raw passion of his kiss. A low moan escaped his throat, and her heart raced at the vulnerable sound. As his demanding tongue caressed along hers, her legs weakened. He held his muscular body against her, pushing her into the wall, and broke the kiss with a sharp breath.

"I'm sorry you had to see that, Haley." His glimmering green eyes brimmed with concern. "Stay close to me, okay?"

His whisper sent delicious chills through her, and her tender nipples hardened under her dress with a heated shiver.

"Okay." She nodded, slinking against him, and moved her arms around his neck.

He stared at her lips with heavy-lidded eyes, darkly cloaked in thick lashes.

"Kiss me again," she murmured.

Damian rushed his mouth to hers. He lowered shaking hands underneath her dress, finding her naked thighs and lifted them around him.

Haley kissed him back, matching his intensity as she squeezed him tightly between her legs. He pressed his hardness into her, pulling up her dress so that his jeans rubbed against her bare sex. She moaned, tilting her hips toward his forceful pressure, and he groaned into her mouth.

Damian pulled back from her embrace, letting her legs find the floor before he stepped away.

He cleared his throat and dragged his hand over the back of his head. "I have to do the ritual."

She nodded, leaning haphazardly against the wall, chewing on her tingling lower lip. She brushed away a wispy lock of hair and straightened, adjusting her dress with a frown, still unsure what she wanted from the future dark lord.

Damian turned away from her, then led her back to the wide hall. They left the dark passage, and he brought her to a set of doors. Chanting voices emanated from the other side, the sound increasing as he opened the door, and he gestured for her to follow.

It was a large ceremonial chamber, lit by dozens of black candles that hung in iron holders on the walls. Black-robed figures wearing assorted masks crowded the room, all chanting in another language. They swept to the side when he entered, forming a clear pathway for him.

Damian stopped at a table with several intricately detailed masks spread across it. He chose a simple black one, lined with black lace and black feathered fringe.

"Here." He brought the dainty mask over her eyes so she could see through the oval cutouts and moved his arms around her to tie the ribbons behind her head.

He clasped her hand, taking her with him as he walked toward the center of the room. Haley blinked behind her mask, clutching his palm as the heavily-robed group of masked figures loomed around her.

He halted at the edge of a circular space in the middle of the chamber. "Stay right here." He gave her a serious look.

She felt strange wearing the mask and stared back at him in silence. He had brought her just inside the edge of the circle, oddly on display for the eerie crowd of shrouded figures. Damian waited for her response, and she gave him a slight nod, trying to shut out the awful chanting around her.

He turned and approached the black stone altar inside the circle.

Haley's heart slammed in her chest. A naked woman lay spread-eagle on the stone structure, widening her knees as he moved between them. One of the high priests handed him a devilish black mask with thick horns, and Damian put it on, covering the top half of his face. His mouth set in a somber line, he looked positively evil in the demonic mask, gazing down at the seductive woman spread out in front of him.

Haley couldn't find her breath, sick with dreading anticipation as Damian unbuttoned his white shirt.

The high priests spoke in another language, reciting words from a tattered black book. Four masked women removed their robes and draped their naked bodies around Damian. The women helped him take off his shirt, then ran their hands along his muscular arms and down his torso. Haley's chest hurt at the sight of the other women's hands on him, but she couldn't bring herself to close her eyes.

It was her first brush with actual jealousy. The alien feeling had her adrenaline pumping. Her insides knotted as the lascivious hands ran up his legs and groped over the front of his jeans. Damian brought his hands down to his belt buckle and pulled it open.

No, no, no, no... She didn't want to see this.

He took down his jeans and his boxer briefs and quickly removed his shoes. Eager to assist him, the women took away his discarded clothes and fondled his muscular calves and thighs.

He stood at the altar like a demonic god in his evil black mask, his well-muscled form naked in the dim candlelight. Haley's breath stopped as one of the women approached his heavy cock with her mouth, reaching her hand toward his testicles.

The woman's loud thoughts stabbed into Haley's mind. *"Master, they look so sore. Let me empty them for you..."*

Haley almost gasped at the miserable emotion swirling in her chest but remained uncomfortably still as the woman slid her mouth over the tip of Damian's cock.

He pushed her away, seemingly irritated by her forwardness, and the girl scurried to kneel at the back of his leg, then lightly massaged his calf in remorse. A trickle of light shone through Haley's savage jealousy.

Damian took a black candle from the high priest and poured hot wax in a small circle over the belly of the girl on the altar. She tilted her pubis toward him with a moan, and Haley cringed, pressing her lips together.

Damian gave the candle back to the priest and took a long dagger from him. He hovered his hand above the naked girl and sliced into his palm. His blood ran in drops inside the wax circle on her stomach, and she undulated her hips off the stone, giving him sensual moans of satisfaction.

The chanting in the room grew louder as the girl sat up from the altar, gazing up at Damian as he stood over her.

Oh my God, he's going to fuck her. Right in front of me. Haley's unblinking eyes filled with stinging tears.

The girl got down on her knees, joining the other naked women at Damian's feet, and bowed low to the ground.

Haley glanced around the chamber as every figure in the room bowed to him. She looked toward Damian and found him staring at her. His horned mask sent chills through her core.

Her gaze dropped to the naked women, literally thrown at his feet. *Am I meant to bow to him as well?* She caught a little smile on his lips. *The devil is smiling at me.* Her heart was in her throat. The chanting came to an abrupt stop, and a dead silence fell over the room.

"May we rise, Master?" The high priest spoke to Damian with his face still low to the floor.

"Yes."

The room erupted with the sound of rustling robes as the masked figures stood and slowly filed out of the chamber.

The women hadn't moved from their places on the floor, and Damian stepped around them, taking his folded clothes from the high priest. He wrapped a strip of black silk around his bleeding hand.

Haley folded her hands at her waist as he approached. His emerald eyes bored into her from behind the demonic mask.

"Your thoughts are inexplicable."

"Oh." She breathed in quietly, catching a glimpse over his shoulder of the naked women as the high priest escorted them to the door. The tightly wound coil inside her relaxed a little at the sight of them leaving.

"Ohh…" Damian kept his eyes on her. "You want me all to yourself, Haley?"

The solid doors closed, and Haley flinched, alone with him in the chamber. He took off the frightening horned mask, turning to place it on the altar.

"Is that your harem?"

A smile spread across Damian's handsome face as he pulled on his boxer briefs. "You've lived with me for weeks, I think you'd know if I had a harem."

"I was guessing you might inherit it with the throne." She worked to keep her voice matter-of-fact. "And I have accidentally witnessed you...bedding multiple women before."

Damian stepped into his jeans and pulled them up with a furrowed brow. "You were watching? I thought I imagined that."

Haley pushed the image from her mind, crossing her ankles where she stood, wringing her hands together. She looked away from his flexing muscles as he shrugged into his collared shirt.

"Are you jealous, Haley?"

She opened her mouth, refusing to meet his gaze. "I don't know. I don't think so. I've never been jealous of anyone before." She lowered her voice, feeling braver behind the mask. "It's absurd," she breathed, "but I guess I don't like to see you with other women."

Damian buttoned his shirt as she swallowed deeply.

"That isn't a problem." He adjusted his sleeves at his elbows. "Since I can't seem to get it up for any other woman." He bent and put on his shoes.

Her lips parted in shock.

He stood up, watching her. Suddenly remembering the mask, she slipped it off, bringing her hand to her hair, and kept her gaze lowered. Her thoughts traveled to images of him refusing the woman's mouth during the ritual. He hadn't been erect. Even hanging limp, it was still rather large. She abruptly halted her train of thought when she felt Damian lingering inside her head, witnessing her dwell on the size of his cock.

He had an amused expression as he took her arm, leading her to the door. "It doesn't look like that with you. You get me painfully hard."

Her steps slowed at the effect his words had on her, a clenching deep in her stomach.

"But my cock remains untouched." He smirked, opening the door for her.

She forced her whirlwind emotions to settle as she moved past him into the giant hallway. The red sky above the high glass ceiling darkened with black clouds that cast a dismal shadow across the wide space.

As they headed down a familiar hall, they walked by the dark passageway where he'd kissed her before the ritual. The memory of his overwhelming body heat pressing her against the wall sent her nerves into overdrive. The ache between her legs was becoming a constant dilemma.

Her muscles tensed as she passed through the large demons guarding the staircase and followed him up the steps. The black marble floor in the hall had been cleaned, leaving no trace of the earlier incident with his brothers, and the corridors were silent and empty. He led her inside the grim room with the creepy furniture. Relief flooded through her as he latched the iron lock behind them. The red Les Paul guitar against the wall caught her eye again.

"What is this room?"

"My bedroom. Or it was until I was seventeen."

"Did you always bring women in here to spank them?" She glanced up at him with a trace of a smile as he walked past her.

Damian sank down onto the side of the enormous bed. "I think you're enjoying those punishments a little too much."

She squirmed at the nagging sensation between her legs. "Will you ever let me…" Her hips shifted as she tried not to clench her thighs together. "Finish?"

"Are you uncomfortable?"

"Yes." Haley took a frustrated breath as a smile crossed Damian's face. "It's very unpleasant." She tried not to mirror his infectious smile.

"That ache?" His gaze wandered slowly down her body.

"Yes." She folded her arms over her middle. "And you tore off my panties."

"I prefer you without any panties on."

Heat flushed her cheeks, and she lowered her hands, walking toward him. Her voice dropped to a silky murmur. "But you've left me so…exposed."

Damian moved his hand just under her dress to her thigh and drew her closer. She brought her knee onto the bed beside him, then straddled his lap. Gazing at him with dreamy lust, she gently ran her fingers over his head. He stared into her eyes as her fingertips went to the side of his face.

"Is it okay if I kiss you?" she whispered.

"Fuck, Haley." His quiet voice came out strained. "What are you doing to me?"

Her lips closed gently over his, stroking his lips with her own, and she slipped her tongue into his mouth, sliding it along his.

There was a sharp knock at the door. "Master? Your father is waiting to speak to you."

Damian pulled away from her mouth. "You've put a spell on me, witch."

She shook her head and tasted her bottom lip, wet and prickled with sensation. There was another rap at the door, and Damian helped her onto her feet as he got up.

"I'll be back as soon as I can." He dropped a thoughtful kiss onto her bare shoulder. "Bolt the door while I'm gone, and don't open it for anyone, including me. I can open it on my own."

Haley nodded, taking a deep breath. He disappeared out into the hallway, firmly closing the thick door behind him, and she slid the iron bar across.

He'd waited to hear the lock successfully latch before starting down the hall, and his presence moved farther away. She turned around, studying her dark surroundings in closer detail. Damian's childhood bedroom.

It didn't resemble anything childlike at all. Almost like a medieval lair with its gothic furnishings and satanic carvings in the dark bed frame. Waving her fingers at the black candles around the room, she lit them all with golden flames in an attempt to brighten the windowless space. She discovered a door, ajar in the shadows that led to a small bathroom.

She used a washcloth to clean between her legs. To her surprise, she didn't linger there, briskly washing and moving down to her inner thighs. Perhaps Damian was right when he'd said she was enjoying his punishments. Her entire body flooded with delicious tension at just the thought of him. It wasn't just the climax she craved, it was *him*, and the skillful way he could bring her to mind-numbing sexual heights.

She left the bathroom, going over to the desk made of knotted dark wood. Curiosity told her to open the drawers and see what the son of Satan could possibly have inside his desk, but she resisted the urge. She moved on to the beautiful guitar that kept drawing her attention and picked it up. Sitting on the edge of the bed, she held it across her lap.

She'd always loved the sound of electric guitar. After her parents were killed, she'd taken lessons, finding the music cathartic, and she'd played random chords in her bedroom for hours. As she grew more sociable in high school, she'd gradually lost touch with it before she'd quit playing altogether.

The deep red Les Paul was a sexy instrument, and her stomach tightened at the realization that Damian must play guitar. The image of his masterful fingers playing the strings sent a flutter deep in her lower core, and Haley carefully set the guitar back where she'd gotten it.

She crawled onto the giant bed and closed her eyes. A golden light flashed in her mind, glowing directly underneath her. She leaned over the side of the bed, spotting a black drawer handle built into the bed frame.

Damian might be the dark-lord-in-training, but he still deserved his privacy.

Hmm... Her powers had pointed her toward the drawer for a reason... *It could be full of body parts or something.*

A chill crawled down her spine. Though it seemed like she could see straight through to his heart, she didn't really know Damian at all. His charms were blinding her to the reality of their situation. She climbed down from the bed and glanced toward the door, trembling at the thought that he might open it at any second and catch her poking into his dark secrets.

She slid the drawer open a few inches, and her pounding heartbeat fluttered with relief. *He did say he was a teenager when he had this room.* Three pornographic magazines, the one on top had a picture of a busty schoolgirl wearing pigtails on the cover. The other two were of a light bondage fetish variety, pretty women with their wrists bound and black ties gagging their mouths. Haley slid the magazines aside. A pair of metal handcuffs, light whips, a riding crop… She picked up the black riding crop, feeling the cool severity of the leather between her fingers.

She snapped the thick leather square against the top of her thigh. It was a pleasant kind of shock. The sound was more startling than the actual sting. Wielded by his hand, it might even be satisfying. She put it back in its place, the urge in her clit more demanding than ever, and took out the schoolgirl magazine, tossing it onto the bed before closing the drawer.

Her torn panties still lay on the floor in the middle of the room, and she collected them, then separated them into two strips of black ribbon. She pulled her hair into two pigtails at the crown of her head, tying them with black ribbon bows, and waited for her new master to return.

CHAPTER NINE

Damian made his way back to his old bedroom, his mind plagued with grim thoughts after the conversation with his father. The remaining rituals would take days to complete, though most were used more for their theatrics than for obtaining the dark power. Lucifer had chosen to eliminate the others and simply complete the last crucial ceremony, which was to be carried out the following day.

In less than a day, he would step into his new role of leadership. Though his father was adamant that he'd remain the final authority on all major decisions made, Damian would technically be the reigning power in Hell.

And she'd be gone.

He didn't want to think about her leaving. She felt like a bright light, shining into the darkness of his existence. Even strapped to Marybelle's table, he'd never felt as weak as he did with Haley on his lap. His swollen testicles were in a constant state of anguish, and his desire for her soft little curves was driving him out of his mind. Yet he craved the torment, the sliver of hope that she would concede to more than just his hands and mouth on her.

Using his mind power to slide open the lock, he worked to shed his dark emotions. She was sitting up against the headboard, her hair done up in sexy pigtails and her ankles crossed, mindlessly twitching her high heels as she thumbed through the pages of a pornographic magazine he'd forgotten he even owned.

Damian broke into a smile when he noticed the schoolgirl on the cover of the magazine in her hands, clearly the inspiration for Haley's choice of ribbons in her hair.

"Someone's been exploring." He walked to his desk and set down a handful of loose scrolls his father had given him to read before the ritual.

She didn't reply, closing the magazine, and climbed off the bed. Damian sat down in the sturdy desk chair and quickly skimmed one of the papers.

"What's that?" She glanced at the foreign words written on the unrolled parchment.

"The text that will be recited at the next ceremony."

"Another ritual."

Damian caught a hint of something in her voice and looked over at her, her thick hair tied into pigtails sent a maddening rush to his groin. "I'll read these later. Are you hungry?"

Haley eyed the scrolls with pouted lips and nodded slightly.

"What's on your mind?" He slipped his fingers around her inner thigh, bringing her closer and swiftly pulled her onto his lap so that she straddled him. Her eyes glazed with arousal, and she kept them lowered to his chest, resting her palms on his shoulders.

"I thought you could read my thoughts."

"I'd rather just hear it from your mouth." Damian played with one of her soft pigtails.

Her gaze drifted to his. Conflicted emotions displayed across her delicate features.

"Um…What do you have in your desk drawers?"

An easy smile spread over his lips. "As if you don't already know."

Her cheeks flushed red. "It wasn't my intention to look in the drawer under your bed."

Damian nodded disbelievingly, recalling what things he kept in that drawer. Whips and handcuffs. "You don't appear to be turned off by what you found in there."

"I think your punishments have put me into some kind of heightened state of mind." She shifted on his lap.

"You're suffering?"

She met his gaze. "Terribly."

Fuck, so am I.

"Tell me what you want me to do to you." Damian rested his hands on her bare thighs, inwardly begging her to let him use his aching cock.

"Put me out of my misery."

His breath was coming in rapid succession as adrenaline pulsed through him. "Be more specific."

She opened her mouth and took in a breath. "I can't."

His ears were ringing with anticipation. "What's holding you back?"

"I—" She glanced away from him. "I don't know. You're the one in control here."

Boy, was she fucking wrong about that. "You want me to let you have release."

"Yes."

Damian pulled down the zipper at the back of her dress and brusquely lifted her off his lap. He stood up in front of her.

"I want to see you naked." He forced her dress down until it drifted to the floor, and her rosy nipples hardened. Reaching behind her, he brushed the scrolls aside, then sat her on the edge of the desk wearing only her high heels. His hands went to her pigtails, pulling at the ribbons, and her wavy hair tumbled down over her shoulders.

"Fuck, you're beautiful."

He heard her breath catch and leaned his face toward her neck, nuzzling into her silky hair, and gently kissed her throat.

He moved his hands between her legs. "Spread these for me."

Haley instantly obeyed, opening her knees. Damian let out a rough breath and slowly slid his fingers into the wetness. He stroked her with them, teasing the sensitive spots inside her.

She lifted her arms around his neck. "Please, Damian… Please let me come this time."

His vision darkened as sharp tingles prickled through his aching groin at her agonized plea. *My poor cock.*

"No." He ran his thumb over her plump clit, and her body shuddered.

Haley leaned back to face him and bit her bottom lip, giving him a pleading look.

He held her gaze for a moment, lost in the sparkling depths. "God, you could make me do anything with those eyes."

114

She gasped, lowering her lashes. He narrowed his eyes at her and fucked her harder with his fingers.

"I'm so close," she breathed. "Please, Damian, please…"

He increased his motions, adding another finger as he pushed them inside her soaking wet pussy. "Don't you dare come, Haley," he growled into her ear, then moved his mouth down to her panting breast and hungrily sucked on it.

"I-I can't, I—" Haley whimpered at his torture. "Please."

She came against his hand, and he shoved his fingers in deeper and faster, stroking his thumb against her pulsing clitoris with each stroke. "I didn't say you could come." He bit down hard on her nipple, and she cried out. He covered her mouth with his and forced his tongue between her lips. He could taste her torment and devoured her mouth until her long climax was spent.

He broke the kiss, coming down from his powerful high. Catching his breath, he pulled his fingers out of her, overcome with the urge to lick them clean, but it would only make his suffering worse.

Her limbs hung loosely around him, and she rested her forehead against his shoulder. A strong feeling of guilt emanated from her mind.

Fuck. I should have given her permission. His neglected cock had driven him to deny her orgasm. "Good girl, Haley, coming for me like that."

She pursed her lips and turned her face toward him. Her intense blue eyes, laden in long, dark eyelashes, held his focus, and a startling emotion he'd never felt before gripped his heart.

"Fuck, baby, I'm sorry." His abs clenched with remorse. "I shouldn't have done that to you. I love the way you come."

Her stiff posture loosened, and she nodded. She looked so angelic amidst their dismal surroundings. He gave in to his urgent desire and kissed her, tenderly grazing his mouth against her sweet full lips. The shocking warmth swirled in his chest again, and he drew back from her, studying her delicate features.

The corner of her mouth twitched, and she looked away.

His gaze sharpened on her. "You're using your magic on me."

She gasped and shook her head. "You know I'm not."

"Then what are these strange feelings you keep provoking?"

Haley paused for a moment before glancing away from him.

He leaned closer to her as she avoided his gaze. "Answer me."

Lowering her thick lashes, she gently took his hand in hers and started caressing her thumb along his. "Maybe you're falling in love with me."

Her words felt like a kick to his balls. He stared at her in silence as he let them sink in.

With a hint of a smile, she released his hand and tapped the desk drawer. "You never told me what was in these."

Damian pulled himself out of his trance and worked to slow the adrenaline speeding through his chest.

Clearing his throat, he pulled the handle. "I was seventeen the last time I lived in this room, so…" He sifted through the contents. "A few joints, a lighter…Tolkien book…"

"Wait… A Tolkien book?" She met his gaze, and a slow smile spread over her lips. "Are you a nerd for Lord of the Rings?"

"I'm not a nerd." He closed the drawer. "I just think he's a good writer."

Her lovely smile spread wider.

"If you wanted to know what was in the drawers, you could have just opened them."

"No, I don't want to go through your things." She slid her gaze to the side. "I know I sort of…did…but I didn't want to…"

Bathed in the curious warm emotion and still reeling from her insane remark about him falling in love with her, Damian swept her long wavy tendrils away from her face.

She studied him, quiet for a moment. "Were you really whipping girls with a leather crop when you were seventeen?"

"It was consensual." He hooked his arm under her knees and helped her to her feet. "I would never do that to you."

"I already like it when you spank me… I guess it's kind of along those lines."

His cock twitched, still raging with painful arousal. He couldn't take any more of her teasing. "Let's go home." His tone was laced with a sinister edge.

Haley eyes flashed. "I don't think I want any more punishments tonight."

"I'm not gonna punish you, sweet girl. I feel guilty enough as it is." He snatched her dress from the floor. "We're both hungry. I liked my breakfast this morning. Maybe I'll eat my dinner off you as well."

Heated desire flickered through her sapphire-blue eyes as she inched the confining material up her hips and pulled it over her breasts.

He stood behind her and grasped the strained zipper closure. "Let's get you out of this dress when we get home. Into something more comfortable for you."

She nodded, lifting her hair so he could zip it all the way to the middle of her back. Her voice fell to a faint whisper. "You should take off your clothes too."

He halted. A dizzying relief washed over him as he held onto her zipper. "Are you sure about that?" He trailed his fingertips along her back.

"Yes." She lowered her head. "But…you're not…just gaining my trust so you can eventually torture me, right?"

He forced the tiny zipper upward. "Why do you think I took off the collar?"

Haley kept silent for a moment, then spoke in a soft voice. "To be honest…" She took a shaky breath. "I'm not very experienced with men."

His heart started beating faster. He cloaked his arms around her and buried his face in her hair. "You don't have to be afraid of me."

She leaned back against him. "I've never felt like this with anyone before. I don't really know what these feelings are."

He traced his tongue along her ear. "Maybe you're falling in love with me."

She stiffened in his arms. Her breasts slowly heaved up and down.

A smile tugged at his mouth, and he gently snagged her earlobe between his teeth. "Are you sure you're ready for my cock, Haley?"

She turned her head, glancing up into his eyes. "Let's go home."

CHAPTER TEN

Haley held onto the crook of his elbow, and he pushed his hands into his pockets as they headed toward the door of the dark palace.

Her steps slowed as she thought of the dragon's rough reptilian hide between her legs.

Damian looked over at her. "What's wrong?"

She pulled her brows together. "I can't ride the dragon without any panties on."

He gave her a half-smile and lowered his voice. "You'll barely even notice the dragon with my cock buried inside you."

Her lower belly clenched, and her pulse sped up. She struggled to keep a normal pace beside him. "That sounds dangerous." Her voice came out breathy.

"Is that a no, then?"

She broke with a quiet giggle. Her pussy was suddenly aching for his attention.

Damian held his focus on the tall black doors ahead of them. "Do I have to wait until after we're finished eating, or can I make love to you on the dinner table?"

Did the dark-lord-in-training just say he wanted to make love to her? Her legs went weak at the idea of him eating another meal off her naked body.

"The dinner table."

"Master." A tiny demon wobbled up to them. "Forgive me for intruding, your eminence. Your father wants to speak with you right away."

"I've already spoken to him." Damian didn't break his stride.

"Oh, Master, that was before he had an opportunity to meet with your uncle Raden. Now he'd like to talk to you again. He's insisting you join him for dinner."

"I'm leaving for the night. I'll speak to him in the morning when I return for the ceremony."

"Oh, but Master. All due respect of course, but he will surely cut off my head if I return to him with that news."

He glanced over at the hunchbacked demon. "If you don't want to lose your head, don't tell him you saw me."

"Damian."

Haley jumped at the bellowing voice behind them. The foyer grew dark with creeping shadows at Satan's presence. She kept her face turned from the looming figure, holding tightly onto Damian's arm as he looked at his father.

"You and your guest will join me for dinner. Come." His voice sounded as if it were two creatures speaking at the same time, a growling animal and a monstrous man combining their vocal cords to form one chilling sound.

Damian reached across and touched her fingers, still wrapped desperately around his arm, and followed his father.

Though she kept her gaze fixed on her shoes, Lucifer's shadowy figure clouded her mind's eye. Built like his sons (or the other way around), his enormous body was at least nine or ten feet tall and made only of bulging muscle, cloaked in a flowing black robe. His dark power left a trail of shadows in his wake as he moved in silence down the hall. Goosebumps prickled over her skin as an image of his sinister face flashed in her head. He had a thick mane of jet-black hair and oversized reptilian eyes that glowed red and yellow, hollow, seeming to have no depth at all.

They walked into an immense dining room, and Lucifer pulled out the chair at the head of a crowded table. He removed his cloak to reveal a giant set of black wings, bony and tattered, folded onto his back. His wingspan had to be at least ten feet when stretched. Her heart pounded as Damian took out a chair for her, the furthest from the winged monster at the head of the table. She sat down, her eyes perpetually lowered. A glimpse of Raden invaded her thoughts, seated at the table nearby Lucifer with a look of pure delight on his sharp, dark features.

A heavily deformed demon waddled by with a rolling silver cart and placed bowls of broth in front of everyone. The table waited for the dark lord to begin eating before they followed. Haley had no appetite at all. The high priest from the earlier ritual sat directly across from her.

"Not hungry, little beauty?" He slurped his soup.

She politely gave him a hint of a feigned smile. Her legs quivered under the table, and Damian slid his hand onto her thigh. The heat from his firm palm soothed her, and she picked up her spoon.

"Damian, your uncle has confided in me about what you've done." Lucifer's demonic voice rang clearly from the end of the table. "While I might understand your motives, there will nevertheless be consequences."

Damian gave her leg a reassuring squeeze, then rested it on the arm of his chair while his father continued.

"For stealing his most personal slave, you now owe your uncle a great debt, and I'll see that it is repaid. It is decided that Raden will wield the whip for the silent scourging portion of your final ceremony."

Damian stared at the table.

"I shall make it impossible for you to keep quiet, Damian." Raden smiled. "The cat o' nine tails will teach you to steal from me, boy. Since the forty lashes start over for every sound you make, I suspect you should anticipate the event to last several hours."

Forty lashes… Haley gripped her chair, taking in a choked breath.

"As for the female participant required." Raden sneered. "I can think of no one more lustful than the witch who so loved to have me force my cock up her cunt each night. Isn't that right, slave girl?"

Haley closed her eyes as Raden called down the table.

"Then she'd turn around and suck it, Damian. Oh, she was *hungry* for my cock. Do you miss it, slave witch? Do you miss sucking my gigantic cock?"

"The *current dark lord* chooses the participant." Damian glared at his uncle.

"Yes, that's correct, Damian." Lucifer's paranormal voice sent chills through her. "And you are so taken with this one. Who else would you have me choose?"

"Marybelle," Raden growled. "Put him in the ground with *that* witch. That's what he deserves."

"Enough, brother." Lucifer's harrowing command shook the table. "One more taunting outburst toward your future dark lord *or* his precious slave witch, and I'll order his forty lashes administered to you as well."

Haley's uneaten soup was removed and replaced with the main course. She stared at the full plate with a sick stomach. *I'm going to be a participant in the ceremony. What does that mean?*

"A fate worse than death for some." The high priest across from her raised his brows, his lips puckered into a sour smile. Haley closed her mind to his energy, working to keep her thoughts hidden from all the mind readers at the table.

Damian leaned toward her. "Don't be afraid, I'll get you through it."

Her mental walls guarded her thoughts against all except Damian, who never seemed to have difficulty breaking into her mind.

"What's going to happen?"

He cut into a piece of meat and took a bite. After a few moments of resounding silence in her head, Haley pierced into his thoughts. She rushed through his memories, searching for information about the upcoming ritual.

An image of a large coffin plagued his mind. He hoped she wasn't claustrophobic.

Oh shit. Oh no... They were going to bury her alive. She struggled to take a breath, working to appear calm.

Damian dropped his fork abruptly and dragged his hand along the shadow of whiskers on his jawline. *"Did I just see my own thoughts in your head?"*

Haley held onto her chair, afraid she might fall out of it. *"Am I gonna die?"*

"No. I'd never let that happen. If you prefer, I'll choose another participant. This might be for the best though, it's impossible for me to protect you if I'm buried forty feet underground with someone else."

Haley stared blindly at her untouched plate of food. *"We'll be buried together?"*

"It shouldn't be longer than a few hours. We're both meant to survive the ritual, the participant is just described as a lustful creature."

His deep voice in her mind calmed her. Her anxiety began to subside as she resigned herself to being buried alive.

Her stomach tensed into tight, twisted knots at the idea of Raden swinging a cat o' nine tails on Damian. She'd heard of the multi-tailed, barbed whip, but thankfully never had to endure such an intense instrument of pain. This was not how their evening was supposed to turn out. She had felt free and excited for the first time in months, almost happy even. They were supposed to be making love on Damian's dinner table, not sitting with Satan himself at his, and eating with rapist uncles.

CHAPTER ELEVEN

Damian brought his face close to hers, and she looked into his eyes.

"Will you please eat something?"

"I'm not hungry right now."

With a slight nod, he sat back in his chair. Raden should be well sated by the repayment Lucifer had ordered, the chance to publicly inflict extreme injury onto him in the guise of a "cleansing" flogging ritual. If Damian decided to release Haley that night, there weren't likely to be any negative consequences. Except for the stabbing pain in his chest whenever he thought about her leaving.

"Do you want to go home, Haley?"

She turned to him, emotion flooding her bright blue eyes. "Yes," she breathed.

He nodded somberly. He'd lost his appetite. "I don't even know where your home is."

Haley watched him for a moment. "My home? I thought…you meant…your home."

Damian took a long sip of red wine. *"I should have released you a long time ago."* He set the glass down softly.

"But…you said…"

"Raden's getting his forty lashes of payment, he won't be leading any uprising against me. It's safe to bring you home tonight."

Damian downed the last of his wine and stood up with a tightness in his throat. He extended his hand to Haley without looking at her. He had to let her go, she deserved to be free from all of this.

Her touch reflected the slightest reluctance as she took his hand.

"Where are you going, Damian?" Lucifer set down his fork.

"Home." He led her toward the door. "I'll see you tomorrow for the ritual."

"And your slave?" Lucifer narrowed his glowing red eyes. "She'll be here tomorrow as well?"

"Yes. It's been a long day."

"It's about to get longer." Lucifer stood, his bony wings twitching as they stretched out. "Why are we prolonging the inevitable?" He stepped forward and cast a dark shadow over them. "When I created Roman, your eldest brother, I was ready to give my seat on the throne to my son." His wings expanded as he drifted closer, and Haley gasped softly. "Roman wasn't fit to be the dark lord. It took twelve more creations to get you, Damian. You were born to take over the throne of Hell. I won't let you slip away from me."

"I know." Damian tried to keep the annoyance from his voice. "I'll be here tomorrow."

"You're running away with her. With your fucking slave witch."

Haley's eyes widened. Damian saw a vision flicker through her head of herself, tucked away in the mountains, rolling around naked in the snow with him in a magical, wintery scene. The fantasy seemed so real as he watched it play through her mind. The familiar tender emotion swelled in his chest at the sight of Haley on the snow-covered ground, grinning up at him, her naked body pink all over from the cold.

Lucifer growled, staring him down. "The final ceremony is about to begin. I suggest you ready your flesh for your uncle's scourging."

"Now?" Damian slowly shook his head. "No." His heart stung with a renewed sense of loss. He couldn't do the ritual yet, he needed to release her first, make sure she was safe before he let himself be buried. "I'm going home for the night." He started forward, daring his father to move out of his way, but Lucifer didn't budge.

"It's the witch, always twisting your fate." He pointed his claw toward Haley. "I never should have let this whore live." He bared his rows of jagged teeth at her. "I'm going to tear your skin off." Lucifer's wings lifted as he raised both sets of arms and lunged toward her.

Damian quickly stepped in front of her, and his father's powerful fists struck him in the face and abdomen, knocking him to the floor. Haley stood behind him, unprotected and vulnerable.

"I let you have her!" Lucifer kicked his chest. "As your slave, your participant. And you still tried to sneak away with her. To deny your place on the throne!" He pounded his fist into Damian's rib cage and cocked his arm back for another blow.

Haley grasped Lucifer's arm in midair and shone her golden powers into his darkly shadowed muscles. Lucifer shocked her with an electric current and caught her by the throat with one of his lower arms as she fell.

Blind rage surged through him. Damian burst to his feet and smashed his fist into Lucifer's body. His knuckles broke against the iron muscles. He hardly noticed the pain and beat his father's face with severe blows until Lucifer released his hold on Haley's neck. She dropped to the marble floor, and Damian rushed to her side.

"Are you alright?"

"Move aside, Damian." Lucifer wiped a torrent of blood away from his mouth. One of Damian's punches had caused his sharp fang to pierce through his lip. "I will watch her die, once and for all. I want all her skin removed."

Damian rose and deepened his voice to a threatening growl. "You'll have to go through me."

Lucifer advanced toward him.

"Wait!" Haley scrambled up from the floor. "You weren't running away, let's just do the ritual." Her voice caught with emotion.

"Too late for you, witch." Lucifer pointed at her. "I shall wear your skin as a cloak."

The violent, dark power flowed through Damian in a strong current. "I'll destroy you if you ever touch her again."

"How dare you speak to your own father like that." Lucifer's voice wavered.

Perhaps he could deny the throne. At that moment, the only thing he desired was to draw nearer to the witch at his back, to fiercely protect her from ever being hurt again.

Haley leaned up on her toes and whispered at the back of his ear. "It's alright, I want to participate in the ceremony."

She didn't believe he could protect her. She wanted to complete the ritual so she could leave him as soon as it was finished. Of course she just wanted it to be over, the whole experience had been nothing more than a nightmare for her. *She doesn't want to be with you.*

"I'll do the ritual."

Lucifer sneered, turning toward the crowded table. "I feel compelled to take away my son's precious prize, to order her skin be flayed off just before they bury her alive with him." He pointed his bulbous lizard eyes at Haley and chills ran through her. "But my brother will teach Damian a proper lesson with the whip. And rest assured, I will quite literally exact my pound of flesh from this little witch." He ran a clawed finger over his bleeding mouth. "When the time is right. Let's begin the ritual."

CHAPTER TWELVE

Damian followed his father through the palace as the rest of the dinner guests walked behind. Haley kept close to his side without touching him. The black clouds overhead crackled with lightning, and the dark halls sparked with flashes of white light. Tension hung thickly in the air as they filed into the room where the earlier ritual had been held, already crowded with onlookers wearing black robes.

A group of cloaked demons heaved a large wooden frame to the center of the room. They positioned it beside the stone altar. A black coffin, custom built to be wide enough for two people, sat on the altar with its lid open.

The crowd once again formed a circle around the altar, and Damian unbuttoned his shirt with quick, jerking fingers. A high priest handed Haley a folded mass of sheer black fabric, and she studied it.

Naked women swarmed around his feet, rushing to his aid as he wrenched his shirt off. Haley glanced at them with a frozen expression, her breasts rising and falling faster with each breath.

His body vibrated with tension. Damian stared down at his belt, unbuckling it, and undid his top button, then yanked down his zipper. The women reached for his jeans, and he waved them away, instinctively moving closer to the witch. She watched him, awkwardly holding the folded fabric in her hands.

He went to lower his jeans and stopped. "It's not too late. I can take you home right now."

She tilted her face downward. "I know."

He stood in strained silence, his heart breaking further with each second. He wanted to leave for the life they'd seen in their visions.

"Are you sure about this? We can just go."

"Not without a life-or-death fight with your father." Her tone was full of pity, and a shock of self-hatred tore through him.

"I can handle him, Haley." The desperation in his chest caused his voice to break. He sounded weak.

She gave him a reassuring look despite the tears building in her eyes. "I'm ready for the ritual."

The sharp pain in his chest felt like the dagger had been sunk back into the freshly healed wound. Resigned to his fate, he shoved his pants down to the floor, dropping his boxer briefs with them, and handed his clothes to a high priest.

"That's for you to wear." Damian's voice had gone cold as he gestured to the folded garment in her hands. "You'll have to take off your dress."

"Oh."

He moved toward her, and she turned around. She swept her hair aside as he unzipped her dress. His cock hardened at the sight of her bare back.

His erection was annoyingly on display for the entire crowd as he helped her pull the dress down. She covered her breasts with one arm and quickly unfolded the gossamer fabric. It was a sheer, fitted floor-length robe. She slid her arms into the sleeves and wrapped the flowing fabric around herself, still utterly exposed.

Damian kept his gaze on the floor, swallowing the deep hurt. He would need to be a fucking man to make it through this part of the ritual. A soldier. Pushing all thoughts of Haley from his mind, he walked naked to the wooden framed structure and stepped onto the platform.

Raden approached him, draped in a black silk robe and holding the cat o' nine tails whip. He cracked it ceremoniously onto the floor. Haley watched from a few feet away as the cloaked demons bound Damian's arms apart with ropes on each side of the thick wooden beam. He spread his legs, his cursed erection still raging, and they bound his ankles to the frame with coarse ropes, stretched tightly to hold him in place.

A soft chant broke out among the crowd. They lifted the hoods of their robes to cover their heads, leaving their eyes dark with shadows. Haley brought up the delicate hood of her transparent robe.

Damian stared straight ahead, willing his cock to go down, but Haley was still so close, her naked curves haunting his peripheral vision.

The high priest recited the texts from the black book, the lashing was about to begin. He clenched his teeth, trying to think of anything but the witch as his groin thudded with painful desire. *She doesn't want you. She's leaving you behind.*

The chamber grew silent again. Damian drew in a deep breath, bracing his stretched muscles. The leather thongs whistled through the air and struck him, wrapping around his hip.

Haley's perfect tits bounced when she jolted at the impact, and his dick remained stubbornly hard even after the wounding assault. Knowing she was witnessing his humiliation made the torture even worse.

He swallowed deeply in his strained throat, keeping his mouth closed in a firm line. His abdomen clenched tightly as the whip struck him below the waist again, sending a stab of pain through his stomach. The entire room waited for him to make a sound, but he swallowed again, fighting the urge to vomit.

Shiny tears gleamed in Haley's eyes. He wanted her to look away, but she kept her horror-stricken gaze settled on him. The vicious whip was not as painful as the agony of her rejection. He'd recover quickly from his physical wounds, but his heart had never felt such intense torment.

His erection finally subsided as Raden continued to scourge his body, raking striped wounds into his muscles, and Damian remained silent. His uncle's thoughts shouted in anger. He was already eleven strokes in, and Damian hadn't so much as cleared his throat. Raden wound his arm back with a vengeance and rained a storm of lashes onto him.

After thirty-four lashes, Damian's stretched limbs trembled involuntarily, and he worked to steady them. Raden switched to his left hand, crisscrossing the stripes along Damian's back. His vision flashed black as the razor-tipped tails shredded his already torn skin.

Raden panted for breath and Damian peered into his uncle's desperate thoughts with smug satisfaction. Only one stroke remained. If he could elicit even the slightest whimper from Damian's throat, he would have another forty to go. Raden glanced at Haley as she stared at Damian with tear-flooded eyes. An idea crossed his uncle's mind of cracking the whip's sharp metal tips right at her perky breasts.

Damian glared at Raden. He would fucking murder him. Whip him to death in front of the entire room with his own cat o' nine tails if he followed through on that thought. Raden smirked, deciding it wouldn't be such a far stretch from the ritual code to let just one land above the neck.

The whip's tails struck Damian across his face, cutting open his cheek underneath his eye.

The slicing tips fell away from his strained neck, and Haley grasped her chest.

Damian let out a slow breath. It was over, he'd taken the entire lashing in complete silence.

They untied his limbs, and he stood on weak legs, dripping with blood. Fresh tears slid down Haley's cheeks as he approached her. He gently pushed back the hood of her robe and slipped the sheer material off her shoulders. It floated to the floor around her feet.

She clutched her arms over her bare breasts, shielding herself from the sea of eyes on her. With a heavy weight in his heart, he guided her toward the coffin and stepped in. Haley breathed in deeply, then followed him inside and lay down facing him.

Lucifer appeared above them and swiftly slammed the lid shut.

Wet with blood, Damian pressed his beaten body against her in the close darkness. Pressure built in his ears as the coffin sank into the ground, pushed by supernatural forces, plunging through forty feet of dirt and stone. The box stilled, surrounded by dead silence.

"Are you alright?" Her tiny voice sounded distant.

"I'm okay."

Haley sucked in a breath. "That was so horrible." She broke into gentle sobs.

He reached for her, shifting so he wrapped his arms around her. "I've been through worse than that, Haley, I'm fine."

She pressed her face against his throat, crying softly. "You stayed silent. How did you stay silent?"

"If I'd made a sound, it would have started all over."

"But what they did to you…" She breathed a whimper. "I can't unsee it."

He hated hearing the helpless anguish in her voice, and he was the cause of it. "I'm sorry, Haley." His grainy voice was raw with guilt.

"What? No, you don't have to be sorry. I just…"

With a sharp pain in his throat, Damian ran his fingers through her silky hair.

"I want to make it go away." Her voice broke again. "For you, I mean. You must be in so much pain."

He wound his hand into her hair. "I'm finding solace in my lustful creature."

He traced his fingertips down her tear-stained cheek to her chin. "Come closer." He tilted it upward, searching her face with his lips until they rested on her mouth. He moved his tongue between her full lips with sudden need. Despite the searing pain roaring through him, his cock craved her attention, hardening at once as she pressed her naked body against him.

"Please, Haley," he whispered into her mouth. "Please let me inside."

Her fingers slipped to the coarse whiskers along his jawline. "But…you're hurt."

Damian pressed his hardness against her bare thigh. "I am…" He choked back a groan. "Please make me feel better, Haley. I need to be inside you."

"D'anakkis ent eren esservius…" Their surroundings shifted to Damian's bed inside his mansion in Seattle. He was lying on top of her, speaking to her seductively in Trinnian, his demonic language. *Let me inside your delicious pussy.*

"Yes." Haley blurted her reply, barely understanding his words, her legs spreading wide beneath him on the soft comforter.

They returned to the darkness of the tightly enclosed coffin.

"I'm so confused by those visions." She skimmed her fingertips along his chest. "They feel so real."

He took a rough breath. "I don't understand them either."

"They make me want you so badly." She brought her lips to his face and found his mouth, then slid her tongue forward and stroked it against his.

He groaned against her mouth. "You have no idea how much I want you, Haley."

"You can have me." She lowered her lush lips to his neck, softly kissing his feverish skin.

He couldn't breathe. Powerful glowing emotion welled up in his chest as his lust consumed him. He guided the tip of his cock between her legs, easing her thigh up over his torso, and pushed inside of her. Grabbing her ass in a firm hold, he slid her clenching muscles along his length. The intense pain of the friction on his open lacerations combined with the most heavenly pleasure he'd ever felt. He reveled in the closeness with her as their heavy breaths mingled in the suffocating space.

Haley moaned into his shoulder, and his grief became almost unbearable. It was the first and last time he'd ever make love to her.

He groaned. *My heart fucking hurts...* He kept his tender grip on her backside, gliding her up and down. The ache in his chest counteracted the swirling pleasure in his cock. *I don't want to let her go.*

Haley trailed her tongue up his throat. She breathed soft moans, calming his pain.

His lower body rushed with pent-up arousal, ready to explode, but he wouldn't allow himself to come yet, he needed to hear her climax.

With an agonized growl, he leaned in to her ear with panting breaths. "It's never felt this good before." He skated his fingertips across her clit.

She whimpered with a soft whisper. "I'm coming."

Damian exhaled and achieved his own bliss seconds later, his pulsing spasms spurred on by her deep, sexual moans.

As he caught his breath in the small space, he tightened his hold on her warm body. *I've fallen in love with her.*

Haley moved her arms around his neck. "I don't want to leave you."

"Then stay. As my queen."

"I want to…" She paused with a dreadful silence. "I can't."

Though he was still buried inside her, it felt as if he'd already lost her. He slowly withdrew from her body, calmly trying to recover from her words. He cleared his throat. "I know."

She reached for him as he pulled away. "I have feelings for you."

He kept his muscles stiff as she snuggled closer. "But not enough to stay with me."

"I don't belong here," she whispered, "…*you* don't belong here."

"I'm the fucking dark lord, Haley, the *ruler* of this place. Of course I belong here."

Haley didn't answer for a moment. She choked back a sob, and the sound gripped his heart.

"Tell me about the life you'll be returning to." He pulled her close again. "What is your home like?"

"Um." She sniffled a little, pausing. "The Castle. Well actually, Stephen's the one who started calling it that. It's really just a giant brick building."

"Who is that?" Damian grazed his teeth along her shoulder.

"Who?" she breathed.

"Your boyfriend?"

"What? N-no..."

"Liar." Damian grasped her ass in his palm. "I recall a blond boy from your memories, politely fucking you in a tiny bed."

She gasped at his harsh teeth on her neck. "That was Neil. My ex." He began to lick her instead, and she melted in his arms. "I don't have a boyfriend."

"Good. And Stephen?"

"My brother. He's a Healer for Adv—"

He halted when she abruptly cut her sentence short. "Adversus?"

She hesitated for a moment. "Yes."

He dragged his fingers along her bare back. If he had followed through with the plan he once had to join Adversus, maybe he could have built a life with her. Perhaps that's what the visions were, wishful thinking. But his path had already been chosen.

"You have a brother in Adversus, and they haven't come to rescue you?"

"I'm sure they're looking for me."

"The soldiers rarely venture to Hell for anything but information. You would have been here for the rest of your life."

"I was counting on the success of my next escape attempt."

Damian had to smile at that. *Remarkable girl.* It faded quickly when he remembered what he had to do. "I'll be bringing you home."

CHAPTER THIRTEEN

Haley buried her face against his chest. *How can I feel so grateful and utterly destroyed at the same time?*

The box jolted and panic shot through her. She lost her breath as the coffin rose from the ground. The lid opened to reveal a vast throne room, lit by candlelight. She lay still in the silk-lined box for a moment, staring at the elaborate filigree markings on the ceiling.

Damian stepped out of the coffin and slid his arms into a dark cloak. Though his scars remained, he had emerged fully healed, flowing with a malevolent power. He emanated strength.

Haley took his hand and climbed out. He wrapped her in a long black robe, shielding her naked body from the crowd of onlookers.

He sat down on the black iron throne and grasped her wrist, drawing her toward him. She held back her emotions as she settled onto his lap.

The creatures in the room all bowed to him, muttering their praise. Her fantasy had ended. Damian had become the dark lord.

"Leave us." The visible dark power distorted his voice slightly, giving it an inhuman inflection. His subjects hurried to follow his command, and the large room emptied.

"I know I should go home." Haley ran her fingertips along his masculine throat. His dark energy moved under her touch. "I'm not ready to let you go."

He caught her gaze, his beautiful eyes had blackened. "Be my queen."

Lucifer's shadows entered the room, and her muscles went stiff.

"At last." His growling voices echoed. "My son has fulfilled his destiny." Enormous reptile eyes stared directly at her. "Now it is time to deliver yours."

"Your reign is over, father."

"The throne suits you." Lucifer stalked closer. "I may not be lord of Hell, but I carry the dark power it brings. I still control you, Damian, and I've decided to remove the witch's flesh."

"Try."

Lucifer started forward and her entire body tensed.

Damian shot up from the throne, grabbing her before she fell, and abruptly set her in the powerful chair. He advanced toward his father.

Smiling to reveal jagged fangs, Lucifer extended his bony wings and lifted off the ground. Damian grasped onto a tattered wing and snapped it. He closed his hands around his father's throat and wrestled him to the floor.

"You control nothing." Damian's eerie growl sent a shiver through Haley. A dark shadow expanded around him as he tightened his grip.

A crowd of hooded demons flooded into the room. They ran toward Lucifer, and Damian bared his teeth at them.

He released his father and straightened, rolling his shoulders. With a deep breath, he turned to the throne.

"Let's go."

Nodding, Haley hurried down the steps to his side.

"Damian!" Lucifer's voices cracked with his scream. "You signed in blood, my son." He coughed as he struggled to stand. "You are bound by blood."

Haley hid behind Damian's rigid form.

"I wanted you to believe you had chosen this path on your own, but I didn't anticipate the witch clawing her way into your head again. You didn't read the scrolls I gave you? They are the guidelines by which you are to rule."

"I don't need fucking guidelines."

"You came to me, Damian. Broken. Ready to end your own life. Raden had killed her." Lucifer centered his bulging eyes on Haley. "The witch with the royal magic.

The queen. It's her fucking golden powers that get you, boy. They blind you. You begged me to spare her life. In return, you'd ascend to the throne under my terms. You signed in your own fresh blood." He grabbed a roll of parchment from the high priest and gestured toward the dark red stain at the bottom of the paper. "I changed the clock back to the time before you'd joined Adversus. The witch was to live her life separate from you. And you are to rule Hell under my orders."

Damian snatched the paper from his claws and studied it. He shook his head slowly. "Six years from now?"

Haley clutched the robe tighter around herself. The strange visions… Were they memories? Of their future?

"Oh my God."

"Silence, witch!" Lucifer used his four arms to adjust his cloak. "She can still live without her skin, I'm sure. Our agreement remains intact."

"You will not fucking touch her." Damian gripped the paper in his fist. "She lives a long, healthy life or I'll end us all."

Lucifer gritted his fangs together, an oddly-pitched growl settling in his throat as he glared at Damian. He jutted a black claw toward him. "Your cock shall never touch the queen witch's cunt again, or I will gladly peel her apart in front of you, is that clear?"

Damian clenched his jaw in silence.

"You were not meant to be with her, Damian." Lucifer shoved a hunchbacked demon forward. "Take her to wherever she lives."

Tears filled Haley's eyes as the creature advanced. She reached for Damian's arm, but the hooded demon dragged her backward.

"Wait." She swallowed, desperate.

Lucifer hissed. "Get her out of my sight!"

Damian stood stone-still, refusing to look at her as she stumbled toward the door. The demon prodded her along, and she couldn't tear her gaze away from Damian. The moving shadow surrounding him seemed to darken. The shock of Lucifer's revelation had barely set in. She couldn't just leave him forever. She had to at least say goodbye. It felt like she'd been ripped open and her heart was being torn from her chest.

"Wait!" Haley pushed the monster holding her, struggling to move past him. He knocked her to the floor with a snarl. More demons swarmed around her.

"I need to… I need to talk to him." She fought their clutching hold, but they shoved her through the door, and it slammed shut.

They wordlessly pushed her along, moving toward an approaching high priest in thick velvet robes.

Her legs gave out, and she crumpled to the floor. "Please, I need to talk to him."

The priest knelt in front of her and held her temples with wrinkled hands. "Where do you live, child?"

"Please, just let me say goodbye."

His lips twisted into a small smile. "I will find it in your memories."

She continued to whimper at the shocking emptiness spreading through her as shadowy clouds formed around her.

The billowing darkness faded. Haley blinked away her tears and pulled her knees close to her chest. Sunlight shone into her bedroom, and a light breeze rustled through a tree outside the window. She was home.

CHAPTER FOURTEEN

"Whose house is this again?" Haley studied the gate
as Aimee pulled into the driveway of a large mansion in
North Seattle. She'd seen the iron enclosure before.
Probably another memory from her erased future.

"Noah Andrews, remember? You met him once, I
think. Apparently he's got a rich roommate or something."
Aimee parked at the end of the crowded driveway and
fluffed up her heavy dark locks. "Maybe we'll meet some
hot soldiers."

Haley gazed silently out the window at the familiar
landscape.

"Please try to have a good time at this party, Hales."

"Okay."

"You've been home for months, but it feels like we
never really got you back."

"I know."

"I just want you to be happy again."

Haley nodded with a smile. "It'll be fun."

Aimee winked. "That's my girl."

Haley straightened her short white flowy skirt as
they headed toward the large front door. She breathed in
the warm night air and climbed the front steps. She knew

the house, it held some strong significance for her other self. None of that mattered; this was her reality now. In her other life, she'd gotten herself killed. Damian had saved her from death with his sacrifice. She should be grateful, enjoying her second chance at life, but some days she could hardly breathe through the blinding pain in her chest. It was like Damian had left a gaping hole where her heart had once been. Her very existence seemed wrong.

Loud music and voices blared inside the huge house. A sizable indoor gym had been converted into a temporary dance floor, flashing with colorful lights and hazy with smoke. After a few shots of whiskey, time disappeared, and Haley let the music move through her, soothing her mournful spirit as she swayed her hips, invisible in the dark room.

Hours later, Aimee went upstairs with the guy she'd been dancing with, and Haley decided to find the kitchen in the giant place. Standing in front of the sink, she drank a glass of water. The room calmed her somehow, but the sensation seemed just out of reach. Her thoughts began to turn dark, the cold, crushing depression pulling her under, and she pushed away the feeling. She'd had too much to drink. She needed to sleep.

Warm lips ran along her inner thigh, and she smiled in the darkness. His hot breath moved closer to her sex.

"Let's take these off, okay girl?" Big, brawny hands slid her panties down her legs. "Yeah, you just need a nice hard dick inside you…"

"Mmm."

"I know you've always had a thing for me, Haley." He kissed her smooth skin between her legs and ran his tongue over her pussy. "You're so fuckin' hot."

She still wore her heels. The night's events slowly came back to her, and Haley opened her eyes. Suddenly alert, she sat up, squinting in the dark. A man with thick dark hair pressed his face between her thighs. She gasped and shoved him away. Her powers flashed a golden blaze, scorching his forehead and some of his hair. He shrieked and violently bit down on her soft inner thigh.

"Bitch!" Holding his head, he hit her across the face, and she wobbled to the floor.

She had fallen asleep on a couch in a deserted room in the mansion. The man's deep voice was familiar. His overly large frame loomed over her.

"Talis?"

"You fucking melted my face!" He grabbed for her, and Haley scrambled backward. "Come here, bitch."

She flew out the door and maneuvered through the crowd with Talis close behind. As she swept through the living room area, he disappeared. She rushed to the front door. Outside in the still night, she took long, steady breaths. Her thigh throbbed in pain, wet with blood. She lifted her skirt and cringed at the deep bite wound.

She started toward Aimee's car where she'd left her cell phone. Ginger was in Italy, and she couldn't call either of her brothers. They would have too many questions. She would just order a ride on her phone. Wandering down the driveway, the surroundings sparked an intense longing in her spirit. Emotion choked her throat, and she clutched her hurting chest, trying to block out the feelings.

Metal clanked in the distance behind her, and she turned. Up ahead, the garage door was open and well-lit inside. A blue-and-white 1970's Chevelle sat on a car-lift with the hood open. Damian stood beside it, cleaning his hands with a rag.

Her heart vibrated in her chest. She couldn't move, staring in silence as tears sprang to her eyes. He sifted through tools in the garage, wearing jeans and a black T-shirt that stretched over his broad chest. The muscles in his arms flexed as he worked underneath the raised car. Blinking away her tears, Haley continued to watch him.

She would turn around and leave. That was the right thing to do, never to come near the cursed house again.

Damian glanced down the driveway. He lowered his arms, still holding the wrench, and stared at her for a moment. Her pulse raced as she held his gaze. It probably appeared as if she'd hunted him down.

Talis burst out onto the front porch, flocked by four large men. "There she is."

They sprinted toward her, and she spun away from them, her high heels slowing her run.

"You scarred my fucking face, cunt. Get over here." Talis caught her by her hair and slammed his fist into her cheek.

Pain bloomed across her face, and she dropped to the pavement. Rough hands held her down as the four men surrounded her and Talis roared into her face. "Look what you did!" He grabbed her legs, slippery with blood, and forced them wide apart. "Stupid bitch."

Talis fumbled with his belt and yanked it open. A hand grasped his chin, and his eyes flashed as he was struck from behind.

Damian shoved him to the ground, and Talis fell in a heap.

CHAPTER FIFTEEN

Damian turned to the other men holding her. The darkness inside him had become visible, coating the air around him. The man he had hit was likely dead, he'd felt the spinal cord snap under the blow. Blood streaked along Haley's legs, it had soaked through the edge of her white skirt. The men still hadn't released her. Murderous, Damian glared at them. Noah would give him hell if he killed off four more of his soldier friends, but these fuckers had it coming.

They wisely let go of her and fled, leaving their fallen comrade on the driveway. Haley sat up, holding her face where the fucking coward had punched her.

"You're bleeding."

She nodded. "He bit me."

The wound was somewhere under her skirt. Damian held back a growl. "You were fucking him?" He knelt down, extending his hand toward her.

Her gaze snapped to his. "No." She gripped his palm and rose to her feet. "I was sleeping on a couch."

"Are you alright?"

She stared at her attacker, slumped over nearby. "I think so. Is he?"

159

He shook his head. The look of horror in her eyes sent a stab of guilt through him. "He shouldn't have touched you." He slid his arm around her shoulders, turning her away from the body.

She moved closer to him and lifted her arms around his neck. His vision dimmed as she nuzzled her face against his throat, inhaling at his skin. This was a dangerous path.

"I'll take you home." He needed to complete the task quickly and be done with it.

"Why aren't you on your throne?"

"It's a demanding role, but I'm able to take a break every now and then." He found the place in her mind and focused on it, creating a black cloud around them until they stood in her dimly lit bedroom.

The lights around a mirror above her vanity table cast a tranquil glow. He stepped back from her onto a plush rug. Everything in her room was soft and lovely, like her.

"I'm going back home."

"So you do live there? You live with an Adversus soldier?" Haley slid her skirt up to inspect her wounded thigh, and he looked away.

"Yeah, we've been friends for a long time. I have to go."

"Please don't leave yet." She rushed toward him and pressed her palm to his chest. "H-how are you?"

Damian glanced downward. Fucking miserable, but she shouldn't have to know that. "I'm not as conflicted now that I know the truth about our situation." He stared down at her hand, afraid she could feel his hammering heartbeat. "How are you?"

"I'm..." Haley closed her arms around herself. "I don't know how to feel, actually." Thoughtful, she slipped off her heels. "I didn't get to tell you how grateful I am. Or say goodbye even."

Her words dug into his chest somehow. He didn't want her gratitude. Though he couldn't expect anything more from her, considering it was forbidden. But in another life, their original future, she had fallen in love with him. Or had she? Maybe even then, his feelings were stronger than hers.

"Well. Goodbye."

"Is that it?" She held his gaze. "Our last goodbye?"

His tone hardened. "What difference does it make how we say goodbye, Haley? You would have left me whether my father revealed the truth or not."

"No." Her voice caught with emotion, and she shook her head, gripping her chest. "Damian, no..." She lowered her head, covering her face with her palms. "I didn't want to leave you. I didn't know what to do."

"I know." Setting aside his bitterness, he guided her toward the bed. "Lie down, you're still bleeding."

"Have you been upset with me this whole time?" Haley slid onto her bed. Tears shimmered in her eyes.

He sat on the edge. "No." He lifted her skirt, stained with blood. The wound was deeper than he thought. *Ugh, fuck...* She wasn't wearing any panties. Consumed by the dark power, he'd become more carnal than ever. The idea that another male had been between her legs sent a shock of possessive rage through him.

He got to his knees on the bed, then parted her legs and lowered his mouth to her bleeding inner thigh. Haley stared down at him as he licked along the bite marks, healing her with his tongue. When the wound had closed, he kept licking. Her velvety skin drove him insane. Her supple outer lips were so close to his mouth, and she wanted him. He could sense her arousal. She held her legs wide open for him, drawing him in.

She tugged her skirt higher, showing him her pretty pussy.

With a groan, he drew back from her. "I need to leave."

162

She climbed to her knees. "No…"

He couldn't look at her. "If I stay any longer, I'm gonna end up making love to you."

Haley stared at him for a moment, then moved toward him and reached her arms around his neck. She embraced him tightly, and he closed his eyes as her powerful hold sent tingles through his body.

"Please don't go." Her whisper was muffled against his shoulder. She held him tighter, pressing her curvy body against him.

He gently folded his arms around her. She was torturing him.

Leaning back from him, she slipped her palm along his face, studying his mouth. "I don't think I can sleep without you tonight."

Fuck. His cock was at full attention, pressed against his zipper, and his self-control had wavered since he'd acquired the dark power. "Then you need to put on some fucking clothes, angel."

Her eyes flickered to his at the name. It had slipped out. He'd never called anyone that before. Though she certainly fit the description.

With a nod, she let go of him and disappeared into her closet. Sitting back on his heels, he waited while she rustled in drawers for a minute, then emerged wearing a pair of tight black sweatpants and a small white T-shirt.

The low-cut thin cotton shirt barely contained her bare breasts, and he couldn't help but stare. "Goddamn, your tits are nice," he murmured.

With a trace of a smile, Haley joined him on the bed.

She looked up at him with a vulnerable glint in her eye. "Will you hold me?"

He drew in a breath and nodded.

She swept a strand of hair behind her ear and lowered onto her side. He rested his head on the pillow beside her, lying on his back, and pulled her close to him.

"Do you like being the dark lord?"

He dragged his fingers through her silky red locks. "It's better than the alternative."

Haley softly grazed her cheek along his chest. "The sacrifice you made... I can't ever stop thinking about it." Leaning upward, she brushed her lips over the stubble on his neck. "About you."

His pulse was racing. She was gonna make this difficult. "Now you can live a normal life."

"But I could never be with anyone else. Knowing you're in Hell because of me." Her tongue skimmed across his ear, sending his cock into a painful state.

"This is the only way." He spoke in a gravelly whisper.

She slipped her hand under his shirt, tracing her nails along his abs. "I miss the way you touch me."

"You know I can't touch you, Haley. I'm not meant to have you."

Her fingertips slid downward, skimming along the waistband of his jeans. "Can you touch yourself?"

Damian struggled to breathe, staring into her sparkling eyes. She was breaking his control, and she knew it. Haley took his hand and moved it to cover the needy ache at the front of his jeans.

She caressed her feather-light touch along the back of his hand. "Let me watch you stroke yourself."

His hands seemed to move on their own, unbuttoning his jeans. He hadn't come at all since his intense climax with her inside the coffin months earlier, and his testicles were desperate for release.

She moved to her knees and took off her pants, revealing transparent red lace panties that sat low on her hips.

Damian jerked his boxers lower.

Gazing at his hard length, she massaged her clit through the lace.

He stared between her thighs, grasping his thick cock, and ran his rough palm along his arousal. It wasn't enough. He needed to feel her touch, her hand soothing his pain. He growled in frustration.

"I need more." He stood up, yanking up his jeans. *I'm losing control…*

She got to her feet and clasped his hand. "Wait."

He stared into her eyes, and his gut clenched. He couldn't resist her.

She brought his hand to her lips and slid his finger into her soft mouth.

"Fuck."

Lowering her heavy lashes, she glided her velvety tongue along his calloused palm. His jaw went slack as she licked it with long, wet strokes. She slipped his hand underneath his boxers and wrapped his fingers around his straining erection.

Rocked with an instant urge to come, Damian pulled out his cock and started touching himself while she watched. She lowered to the floor, on her knees in front of him, and brought her mouth to his slick tip.

"No, baby, it's too dangerous." He held her chin with a shaking hand, keeping her lips away from his dripping cock. "Touch your pretty clit for me."

Her eyes hooded as she slid her fingers under her panties and slowly teased herself. His cock swelled with a growing need as he took in the view, and he tightened his grip.

Biting her lip, she touched herself with feverish motions and moaned softly. "I'm so close, Damian... I'm about to come." She parted her lips, inches away from the throbbing head of his cock.

Damian groaned, hardly able to breathe as he stroked his intense need.

Her erotic panting was sending him over the edge, and he ached to shove his dick between her full lips. She whimpered in orgasm, opening her mouth for him.

"Ugh, fuck yes, angel, show me your tongue." He jerked his cock faster.

She did as he asked, leaning closer as he came, gazing up at him as he spilled onto her tongue and open lips.

Damian slowly rubbed his palm along his shaft until the last of his climax was spent. He breathed in deeply and ran a hand over his jaw as she swallowed and licked her lips. He'd just fucking released, and his dick was still miserably hard, ready for more of her torment.

"It isn't enough." Pushing his erection down into his jeans, he zipped and buttoned them. "I can never have you like I need you." He sank down into an armchair, lowering his head, and gripped his temples.

Haley stood up from the floor and pressed his shoulders back against the chair. She climbed onto his lap, straddling him, and her long silky hair fell softly around him. Taking his hands in hers, she moved them up her body, over her thin shirt, across her perfect tits.

He let out a rough breath as desire burned through him. "Why are you doing this to me?"

Her hand wandered downward between them, and she rubbed his achingly hard cock through his jeans.

"You know the fucking rules, Haley."

"I don't care." Her breathy voice was tender with arousal. "I need to feel you inside me." She leaned toward his ear and caught it gently between her teeth.

He growled at her, darkness pulsing through him, and grasped her luscious ass in a wringing grip.

She arched her back so her tits lifted toward his face and pushed him further, sliding her lace-clad pussy along his lap.

His sense of control snapped. He stripped her shirt over her head, and her tits bounced, suddenly on display for him. Beyond rational thought, he closed his mouth over her pink nipple, hungrily sucking it. He groaned, pulling away before he drew blood.

Damian stood and grabbed her wrist, drawing her toward the bed. "You want me to fuck you?" Snatching a hairbrush from the vanity table, he spun her around and gave her ass a few hard smacks with it. "Get on the bed." His voice didn't sound human.

With a hint of reluctance, she followed his command. He pinned her wrist to the white iron headboard, then wrapped her T-shirt around it and cinched it tight. She stared at him with glittering sapphire eyes as he jerked his own shirt upward and took it off. He swiftly tied her other wrist to the headboard with his shirt and shifted his focus to her panties.

Despite the flash of fear in her eyes, Haley parted her legs for him. He grabbed the red lace, his hands cloaked in dark shadow, and ripped her panties apart. The evil force roared through him, mingling with his suffocating lust.

He pushed her torn panties between her lips, into her mouth, and grabbed the hairbrush. "Show me your clit, dirty girl."

She spread her legs wider, and he slapped his fingers between them.

Her panties muffled her soft moan, driving him further into madness. He swatted her clit a few times with the back of her hairbrush and then turned it, assaulting her pussy with the bristle side. Her naked breasts heaved as she tilted her tender sex toward him.

Damian rubbed the bristles along her clit, and she whimpered, her toes curling into the comforter.

With a growl, he advanced, crawling over her until his face hovered above hers. "You belong to me, beautiful angel. Understand?"

She nodded, staring deep into his eyes.

"Good." Damian kissed her neck, then nibbled and sucked hard enough to leave a mark.

He shoved the ribbed round handle of the hairbrush inside her, and she moaned around the lace in her mouth. He kept thrusting, working it against her G-spot inside her.

He dropped his voice to a hoarse whisper. "You're mine, naughty girl." He dragged his tongue up the side of her throat.

Her eyes went glossy as she rode her hips with his harsh thrusts. He groped her tits with his other hand, then glided his fingertips down across her sexy scar, and she flinched.

"Beautiful siren." Damian caressed her reddened clitoris instead, and she widened her legs for him while he glided the hard handle in and out of her.

A tap at the door jarred him from his trance, and he halted, holding the brush handle deep inside her.

"Haley?" A male stood in the hallway. "Can I come in?"

Damian gently pulled the red lace out of her mouth, and she swallowed, still tethered to the headboard.

"No, I'm…" She licked her lips. "I'm just really tired, sorry Adam."

"Oh sure. Hey look, I'm heading out on a mission. Be gone for a few days. You gonna be alright here by yourself?"

"Yes, I'm fine." Haley cleared her throat lightly, her breasts steadily rising and falling.

"Well, you let me know if you need anything."

"Okay. Be safe."

"I will."

The man's footsteps moved down the hall, and Damian leaned in close to her face, working to control the violent anger speeding through his veins. "Who the fuck was that?"

"My brother."

His jealousy faded into guilt as he realized he still held the hairbrush between her legs. He slid it out of her and tossed it aside. Haley glanced at it with a little smile as he untied her wrist.

"Wh—I thought…"

"That was a risk, Haley." He unknotted his shirt from her other wrist, trying to ignore the powerful ache in his groin. "I shouldn't have done that."

"But…" Unbound, she sat up, and her tits jerked with the sudden movement, drawing his focus.

He pulled his T-shirt on and got to his feet. "I can't handle being around you. This has to be the end."

"No. Please…" Moving to her knees, she clutched her hand between her breasts.

He forced out a breath. "You know this is dangerous, baby. We can't keep—"

"I can't do this anymore, Damian." She shook her head. "I'm so fucking broken over you." Her tiny cry tore into him. "Why did you change my destiny?"

Trying to breathe through the crushing weight on his chest at the sight of her tears, he slid his hands into his pockets. "I can't live without you."

Haley cleared her tears as more fell from her shining eyes. "You already are." She hung her head low and covered her eyes with her hands, quiet for a moment. "I need you."

Her soft whisper broke him inside. *What can I do?* The only other option was death, and the blood-signed contract proved he couldn't handle that.

"Just live your life." He sat down beside her, pulling her into his arms. "I need you to do that for me, baby. Otherwise, all of this was for nothing."

"This is dark magic. There must be a way out."

"Lucifer will take any opportunity to torture you in front of me, Haley. He won't let you die until he's torn you apart." He caught her chin, tilting her face toward him. "Don't make me go through that."

Her lower lip trembled. "He's gonna torture me whether we follow his rules or not."

She was right, they'd been completely fucked from the beginning. Because of him. He released his hold on her, then turned, staring at the floor.

"I could visit my aunt's coven in Florida. There might be a spell or—"

The satanic force inside him slaughtered any gleam of hope. "Leave it alone, Haley."

His stern command struck her silent.

His stomach twisted at her downcast expression. "I'm not trying to be harsh."

She nodded and brushed a tear from her cheek.

His chest ached. He hated seeing her cry. "It won't hurt forever." His voice hitched as his throat swelled shut, and he swallowed hard. "You'll move on. You'll be alright."

"No…" She looked over at him. Her teary eyes had turned crystal blue. She drew in a deep breath. "I'm in love with you, Damian."

The strange tender emotion he'd been longing to feel again seeped through the heavy darkness inside him. It spread deep in his heart, easing the relentless pain he'd endured there since the demons dragged her away from him.

"I love you too, angel." He climbed to his knees on top of the bed and cloaked his arms around her, nestling his face against her neck.

"I'll do anything to keep you close, Damian." She moved her palms to his chest and gripped his shirt in her fists. "Even if it means I have to kill Lucifer."

His heart pounded as a fierce glowing heat spread through him, warring the evil inside him. *My little assassin angel.* He was supposed to be keeping her safe, not the other way around, and murdering his father wouldn't eliminate the supernatural contract, per the fine print.

But maybe she was right. It was time to fight back.

"One step at a time, baby." He laid her down onto the pillow and cuddled close to her, enveloping her naked body. "Get some rest. Tomorrow we'll visit your aunt's coven."

CHAPTER SIXTEEN

The miserable ache in his chest had lowered to his groin. She was so close and yet forbidden. He couldn't handle another night like that, not with the dark energy ripping through him, fraying his willpower.

Fresh from her shower, she loosened the towel in front of him and slid a soft white sundress over her head, wearing nothing underneath. Painful, desperate desire tore through him alongside the dark current. She stepped into a pair of wedge heels and bent over, tying the dark blue cotton ties around her ankles.

He couldn't look away from her, grappling with the intense urge to strip her naked and spank her for teasing him.

She straightened, smoothing her dress and caught his gaze. Her eyes glimmered with a sudden arousal, and she glanced downward.

So fucking innocent. "You're torturing me."

Haley gave him a tender look. "It's okay, baby. We're gonna make it through this."

The look in her eyes made him half-tempted to believe her. He couldn't bring himself to reply. There was probably no point in going to see the coven, but she was so optimistic. He had to at least try for her sake.

"Because we're together." She held his gaze.

His chest tightened at the gleaming hope reflected in her eyes as the wicked force raged inside him. Truthfully, he was out of options. If he attempted to murder his father and failed, he'd be doomed to watch her be flayed, and he couldn't endure that, but he'd most likely have to at some point. His lungs seized at the thought of it.

"You're right, angel."

She gave him an adorable half-smile. "Ready?"

"Yeah." He swallowed past the lump in his throat.

Damian pulled her into his arms and let the black energy engulf them. The throne's power seemed to grow stronger each time he used it. The darkness disappeared from the air around them, and they stood before a massive gray house on a secluded property. Horses grazed in a grassy field behind the house.

Haley moved to his side and grasped his palm. He squeezed her hand, drawn to her warm touch. The evil shadow inside him seemed almost visible in the bright sun.

As they approached the front porch, the back of his neck prickled, and he ignored it. He doubted there could be anything inside the ranch house worse than he'd already seen in Hell. His instincts had most likely triggered because of past fears. Meeting an entire coven of witches had always been one of his worst nightmares.

Another chill ran through him as he pressed the doorbell. No witch's powers could compete with what resided in him now. He toyed with Haley's long strands of cinnamon-red hair. The silk between his fingers calmed him.

The door opened a crack, and a young woman peered through the opening. The thick frames of her glasses hid light-blue eyes. She swept her dark-red hair away from her forehead, squinting in the sunlight. "Haley?"

A smile broke over Haley's lips. "Emily."

"Oh, my gosh, this is a surprise." She glanced toward Damian and darted her gaze away. "Uh, come in."

"Thank you. I'm sorry to drop in like this. I didn't have your number."

"No problem." Emily fidgeted with the sleeves on her dress as they walked inside. "It's been so many years."

"Is someone here?" Another young woman entered the foyer, adjusting the cleavage of her red bikini. She teased her long blond hair with her fingers and caught sight of Damian. "Oh, hello." Her green eyes sparkled as she stretched her hand toward him. "I'm Cassie."

He kept his hands in his pockets, and Emily spoke up.

"This is, ah." She gestured toward him, keeping her gaze downward. "I'm not sure exactly. He's with our cousin, Haley."

Cassie looked toward Haley. "Oh my gosh. I didn't even see you there." She hurried forward and pulled her into a close hug. "Your man is huge. He fills up this entire room."

Emily gripped her hands together and tilted her head toward a large sitting room. "Come in. Have a seat."

Cassie followed her. "Yeah, are you thirsty? We've got beer, iced—"

"We're looking for Collette." Damian tensed his grip on Haley's hand, drawing power from her palm as he buried the uneasy feeling.

"Oh." Cassie's smile faded.

Haley released his hand and cupped her arm around his middle. "Sorry to be so abrupt. We do need to see Aunt Collette as soon as possible."

"Well, you've found me." A blond woman swept into the room wearing white shorts and a black tank top. She looked as if she could be Cassie's slightly older sister rather than her mother.

"Haley, my love." Collette stretched her arms toward her, and Haley slipped away from Damian to embrace her aunt.

"Why did she seat you in here?" Collette shot Emily a look. "This room is awful, let's go to the sunroom. Follow me upstairs."

Damian weaved his fingers through Haley's and caressed his thumb across her skin as they walked after Collette. Emily and Cassie followed, climbing the stairs behind them. Blocking the exit. There didn't seem to be malicious intentions in the witches' heads, but they were all able to read each other's minds, working to keep their own thoughts hidden.

"This is my favorite room in the house." Collette led them toward a bright doorway at the end of a dim hallway. She sighed and draped herself over the arm of a thick couch. Sunlight beamed through glass windows covering the far wall and half of the ceiling.

Damian turned as Cassie and Emily entered the room. Haley wasn't there. His heart slammed in his chest as he searched the space.

"Where is Haley?" he growled.

"She went to find something." Cassie dropped into a wicker chair.

"It's all right, Master." Collette winked. "She's just exploring, searching for the solution to your problem. You're meant to stay here while she finds the answers you came for." She patted the cushion beside her. "Sit down with me."

The hallway was empty. Haley had vanished.

"She really is okay." Emily shifted the collar of her dress. "She'll come back."

Damian gritted his teeth. The timid one seemed to be the most honest of the three. It might be better to wait a while for Haley to return than go look for her, the entire place could be a maze of illusions.

Collette eyed Emily with a burst of laughter. "Damian can read your mind, honey. Best to hide those dirty fantasies for later, when you're alone."

Adjusting her heavy glasses, Emily sank deeper into her chair, a deep blush running into her cheeks. Aside from seeming extremely nervous in his presence, the young woman had kept her thoughts guarded from him.

"Although Emily…" Collette tapped a finger along her lips, glancing back and forth between Emily and Damian. "You do look an awful lot like your cousin, same coloring, complexion…and those breasts." She turned her attention to Damian. "Don't let that sack of a dress she's wearing fool you, she's hiding quite a little figure under there. Curves in just the right places. Unlike her sister." She rolled her eyes toward her other daughter. "Cassie likes to show it off, but she doesn't have nearly as much to fill out those tiny bikinis."

Cassie stared at her. "You're making him uncomfortable."

"You're doing a fine job of that yourself with your lack of clothing, dear. I can sense his arousal from here. Why don't you just spread your legs so he can get the full picture?"

"I was headed to the pool when they got here."

"Oh, that's all you do anymore. Sunbathing all day long. At least Emily studies the craft." Collette leaned forward, centering her focus on Damian. "Emily seems harmless, but she's very good with spells. Don't be surprised if she puts a love hex on you." She shifted her position on the couch with a girlish giggle. "As you might have guessed, my shy little daughter does not have many lovers. Although, I did catch her once with one of the ritual snakes between her legs."

Emily's head snapped up. "That's not true."

"Oh yes, she was just 'playing' with the snake, just wanted to give it a nice warm home."

Emily opened her mouth with a shake of her head.

"I'm teasing. My goodness, lighten up a bit." Collette breathed in a laugh, gazing at Damian. "It's all right, Emily. I'm sure you've roused the master's lust also. Perhaps he's imagining you and your sister together."

Damian worked to shut out her annoying voice and pushed his hands into his front pockets.

"Or are your fantasies of a more violent nature? Now that you're no longer powerless to our kind." She took a long drink of iced tea. "Maybe he'd like to force you girls to hurt each other."

Her continuous rambling got under his skin. Damian folded his arms and kept his gaze on the empty doorway.

* * *

"Damian?" Haley said his name under her breath. She was alone in the hallway.

The sun-drenched hall ahead had seemed to fade away as the walls twisted around her. Brushing her hair away from her face with a shaking hand, she turned to go back to the stairs, but the hallway consisted of only closed doors now. Steadying her breath, she quieted her racing thoughts. A door opened behind her, and her head spun toward it.

"Sorry. Did I startle you?" A young man stepped into the hall. He licked his lips as a lock of brown hair fell over his forehead. Shirtless, he played with the drawstring on his shorts. "I'm Trent."

Haley glanced up from his firm body. "Do you know where Collette is?"

He paused with a smile and caught his bottom lip between his teeth, languidly gazing at her with dark-green eyes. "Who are you, again?"

"I'm her niece." Haley gave her surroundings another onceover. "Where am I? I was with her a minute ago, and—"

"Easy. Just take it easy." He rested his palms on her shoulders with a gentle touch. "I'll show you the way."

Haley drew back from his soft hold. "Thank you." She spoke clearly, working to eliminate the strange tension.

"This way." He started walking.

Haley followed, studying the long hallway.

"I gotta admit something." Trent grazed his fingers against her arm. "I kind of already knew who you were."

Silent, Haley kept her steady stride beside his leisured pace.

"The queen witch." He adjusted the waistband of his low-hanging shorts, his eyes gleaming with desire, and she avoided his gaze.

Lucifer had also called her the queen. The witch with royal powers, but she'd never heard of any monarchy among witches.

Trent swiftly moved in front of her, and her palms flattened against his abs. She jolted, pulling her hands back.

He breathed a chuckle. "We're going this way." He headed down a shadowy hall beside her. "You know..." He dropped his voice. "You can touch me."

She took a deep breath. This boy set her nerves on edge. The dark corridor appeared endless.

Trent flashed a smile when she didn't respond. "I just meant that I'm not gonna break."

Haley nodded. His thoughts were oddly blank, but his energy simmered with lust.

"Do you like to swim? I'm sure Cassie's got a bikini you can wear."

"No, I'm not here to swim. I need to see my aunt."

He slowed his walk a bit, and she glanced back at him. He seemed to notice her frustration and picked up his pace.

A little color spread across his chiseled cheekbones. "Sorry, Your Majesty."

Her eyes widened.

Trent's thoughts flickered through her head. He readjusted his shorts, itching to reach for his cock. His genitals had been fitted with a steel cage along his length, a chastity device of some kind.

She tried not to cringe and relaxed her pace, holding her arms at her waist. "You don't need to call me that, really."

In the room beside him, a redheaded woman sat on the edge of a bed and turned her face away. Haley halted and double-checked the room, but there was nobody there. She squinted.

"Did you see her?" Trent moved close to her side. "Your mother?"

The confirmation stunned her for a moment. Past wounds split open, bleeding as the familiar sense of loss spread through her. "She's... Was it her?"

"Yeah." He pointed his gaze downward. "She visits here sometimes, it's where she grew up with Collette." He looked into her eyes. "You want to summon her?"

Silent, she stared at him. "You know where she is?"

"Of course." Trent folded his arms over his smooth chest muscles. "The after-place." He grinned. "It's fuckin' awesome."

Haley gaped at him as she took in the information. Did he really know where her mother spent her afterlife?

"You can talk to her. Here." Trent opened a solid iron door a few feet away.

Haley followed him into a low-lit room. There was no furniture, and the hardwood floor was painted with hundreds of black symbols. He took her to the far wall and opened a wood-paneled door, revealing a tiny closet.

"Come on." He slid his fingers along her palm and twined them with hers.

Her senses heightened as warning signals blared in her head. She tugged her hand away from him. "Actually, I'd rather just see Collette."

"Oh." Trent gave a little nod. "Yeah, sure. Sorry."

He led her back out into the hall, walking his odd stride as he brushed his fingers over the trail of hair along his lower abdomen. Farther ahead, a large group of women moved toward them. Some looked to be Haley's age and some much older, all of them wore simple black dresses.

She leaned toward Trent as the women approached. "Is this the coven?"

"Yes."

The witches kept their blank gazes trained on Haley as they passed, and a shiver skittered down her back. Odd for such a large group to be so utterly silent.

Moments later, the sound of her aunt's laughter carried from around the corner and Haley's heartbeat sped up. She rushed toward the sunny room with Trent close behind.

"Haley! What a surprise." Collette beamed at her. "And you've met Trent, I see."

"Yes. And she is…" Trent swept his hand along Haley's forearm. "Just amazing."

Damian's eyes turned black as he studied Trent, and Haley swiftly moved closer to where Damian stood. He clasped her arm in a shocking firm hold and drew her to him. His fingers trailed along her neck and into her hair as he knelt his head and connected his lips with hers. His tongue slid between her lips, and he pulled her closer.

"What a rude thing to do. Honestly."

Collette's voice rang in the back of Haley's mind as Damian slowly wandered her mouth with his tongue. She let the smallest moan escape her throat, and he drew back from the tender kiss. His obsidian eyes shifted into glimmering emeralds again, and she held his deep stare for a moment, shutting out everyone else in the room. He seemed beaten and weary, seeking her affection.

He closed his arms around her. "Don't leave me with these witches again."

She nodded, drawing her brows together.

"Uh, well yes. There was some sexual tension between Haley and me. She came off a bit…shy around me. Especially when she saw the cage under my shorts."

Damian's muscles went stiff, and Haley darted her gaze to Trent, who stood behind Collette, grazing his fingers along her shoulders.

Collette crinkled her nose with a smile. "Did he show you his chastity cage, Haley?"

"Mother, stop it." Cassie gave her a serious look.

"What? So I keep a little cage on my boy-toy." Collette giggled. "Not so little, actually…"

"You saw his cock?" Damian's voice was a low grumble.

Haley quickly shook her head. "No. Well, just in his thoughts, I guess." The shadow inside Damian visibly surfaced, and she flattened her palms on his hard chest, leaning up toward his ear. "Calm down, you know yours is the only one I want."

The dark current flowing along his skin began to slow.

"So, um." Emily's voice squeaked a little, and she paused, studying her nails in her lap. "Did you end up finding what you came for, Haley?"

"What a ridiculous question, Emily." Collette lazily traced her red nails across Trent's abs. "Rest easy, Haley. I've got the whole coven looking for a way out of your little contract with Lucifer. For now, you're staying for lunch."

Turning toward her aunt, Haley clasped her chest as a wave of relief washed over her. "Do you really think it's possible?"

"Without a doubt." Collette puckered her lips and shook her head. "Now, let's get ready for lunch. Shall we take a dip in the pool while Emily prepares the meal?"

Haley's senses sparked, and she slowly lowered her arms. "Oh…no…I'll help in the kitchen." She resolved to brush off the negative feeling and shifted her focus to Emily. "You like to cook?"

"Nonsense, you're our guest!" Collette waved her hand. She shoved her elbow into Trent's side. "You, however, can go sit in the corner for being such a bad boy."

She narrowed her eyes with a little smile. "Showing your dirty parts to my lovely niece."

Damian growled low in his throat, and Emily glanced up at him with wide eyes.

"That never happened." Haley squeezed Damian's rigid bicep, but he kept his glare on Trent. She looked toward Emily, whose face had gone pale. "He's harmless."

Collette snickered. "Our Emily isn't used to so much testosterone. You'll have to forgive her, she hasn't been with a man since she was a teenager, for goodness sake." She ran her fingernails along Trent's waistband. "But one look at this perfect boy, and I had to keep him for myself."

"Mother." Cassie crossed her arms. "Leave her alone."

Emily squirmed in her chair. "No, it's fine."

"You see!" Collette gestured toward Emily. "She doesn't mind! Trent was always supposed to be mine, it was destiny." She jerked his shorts, and he bit his lip with a little moan. Collette winked at Haley. "He always wanted me. Even when he took Emily's virginity, he dreamed that it was me."

Haley gasped. Her heart pleaded with her to stick it out, holding onto the shred of hope that this creepy coven could somehow help her find a way out of the dark, but her pained stomach, twisting into knots, wouldn't let her believe it.

She gripped Damian's arm and spoke into his mind. *"I think we should leave…"*

"Thank God, baby, let's get the fuck out of here."

The sunlight dimmed as a black shadow crawled from the edges of the bright room.

Collette squealed and clasped her hands together. "The guest of honor is finally here!"

Damian groaned. "The bitch summoned Lucifer."

"What?" Haley snapped her gaze to her aunt. Adrenaline pumped through her as a swarm of black clouds flowed into the room.

Damian cloaked Haley in his own darkness, but they remained in the shadowy room. "Shit, he's holding me here." His voice was barely audible through the hum of the static-filled black mist. He stared down at her. "Go."

Collette glared at Damian. "We will not serve a dark lord as powerless as you. Your father is our true master. He will teach you to be a proper leader."

"Go!" He pushed Haley toward the open doorway.

"The witch is mine, Damian." Lucifer's eerie voice boomed all around her.

A shock of pure white light flared, then spread, piercing through the dark clouds. It swirled around Haley until it enveloped the room.

CHAPTER SEVENTEEN

The powerful white light vanished a moment later, and Damian stood in a wide hall, lit by sparkling crystal chandeliers overhead. The vicious dark power didn't course through his muscles any longer.

Haley studied her pale-green silk gown, running her fingertips over the front. She glanced up at him with a pleading look.

Damian loosened his tie. This was the moment she'd been dragged to his uncle's chambers, but there were no giant evil demons attacking her in the hall yet, just the faint sound of the fashion auction nearby.

His father could be orchestrating some ultimate torture for him, making him relive her death for eternity. Fuck, he couldn't go through it again.

"But I remember…dying. In this dress." She clutched the flowing skirt in her palms. "And then…I wasn't dead. And you became the dark lord, and Lucifer…" Tears filled her eyes, and she pinched her brows together. "He's behind this, isn't he?"

He pulled her into a tight hold. "I'm not gonna let anything happen to you."

She sniffled. "Do you still have the dark power?"

"No." His thoughts seemed clearer now that he was free from the throne's shackles. That pure light had been so comforting. It had somehow overpowered his father's shadow.

Haley caught his gaze. Her eyes always turned ice blue whenever she cried. "What should we do?"

He searched his brain for a solution. They could never escape his sadistic father, he would terrorize them forever. Until her final tortured breath.

When he didn't answer, she drifted away from him, searching the deserted hallway around them, her long dress swaying as she walked. That floor-length silk had been the last thing she'd worn in this life.

Damian swallowed hard. He'd actually cried when he'd held her cold body. The grief choked him again, and he took a deep breath through his constricted throat. She was alive, her dress was intact and hanging perfectly on the curve of her hips.

Her death still haunted him. His spirit recalled every crushing second of it, powerless as she had slipped away from her body.

He reached for her hand and clutched it in a desperate hold. Lost in his dark thoughts, he craved a deeper connection with her and looked into her mind. He felt her emotions as the trickle of hope inside her slowly swelled, growing into a powerful faith. Her intoxicating warmth spread through him, soothing his pain, and his breath caught in his throat.

She gazed at him with teary eyes. "I think we're safe, baby."

He dropped his forehead to her bare shoulder and grasped her waist, clinging to her as emotion welled up inside him. He tried to swallow it, but scorching tears flooded his eyes.

Damian knew his voice would come out sounding weak as hell, so he used his telepathic voice instead.

"Please don't leave me again, angel. I'm not strong enough to handle it."

She nuzzled her cheek against his.

He gritted his teeth to fight it, but a cursed sob broke from his throat. *"I fucked up, Haley. I never should have asked my father for help. Now he's gonna torture you to death. I can't go through that, angel. I can't lose you again."*

She drew back from him, and he gripped her tighter, lowering his lashes. As she studied his face, he kept his gaze firmly fastened on the floor and cringed when she reached up and swept her thumb across his fallen tear.

"I know I look like a weak motherfucker right now."

She shook her head. "You're the strongest man I know." Haley moved her hand down to his chest and held her palm against his pounding heartbeat. "You taught me how to fight."

He lifted his gaze to hers and caught the determined gleam in her beautiful eyes.

"Because of you I'm never gonna stop fighting." She took his face in her delicate hands and pulled him down toward her until his forehead touched hers. "I'll always find a way back to you, Damian."

Fresh tears seared his eyes, and he grasped her palm with a shaking hand. "Let's go."

She followed his lead, and he kept a steady pace toward the exit. He brushed his knuckles underneath his eyes as he guided her out the door.

"Where are we going?"

He couldn't answer, his throat felt cinched shut. He strode through the dark parking lot, and she hurried alongside him. He stopped at the driver's side of his Chevelle, snatching the keys from his pocket.

Haley gazed at his car and skimmed her fingers along the chrome trim. "I missed this life."

He felt like he couldn't breathe as he opened the heavy door and slid the seat forward. "I'm gonna fuck you out of that dress."

His statement caught the attention of an elderly couple passing by and Haley glanced in their direction. Damian didn't care about the random strangers in the parking lot.

He struggled to be patient. "Get in the car, baby."

With a hint of a smile, she crawled into the backseat. She inched up her skirt as Damian got in and pulled the door shut. The slit at her thigh climbed higher, and she hooked her thumbs into the top of her panties, sliding them down. He moved his hands over hers and helped her take them off.

The light-mint silk draped along her lap, and she swept it aside, opening her bare legs. "Do you think it's safe? What if your father finds us?"

"I'll protect you." Damian let his hand wander up her inner thigh. His father was the furthest thing from his thoughts.

He touched her velvet-soft skin between her legs, and Haley spread them a little wider.

"I'd die to keep you safe, angel." Venturing between her slit, he slid two fingers inside her.

Her breasts slowly heaved as her breath came faster, and he lowered his face to her cleavage.

"So fucking warm." Damian groaned as a euphoric wave crashed over him. "Let me see you."

She fumbled with the zipper behind her and shifted the tight silk down until her tits came into view. Her skin blushed pink in the steamy interior of the car, and he tasted her rosy nipple while he slipped his fingers in and out of her wet pussy, stroking the sensitive spot inside her with each pass.

Squirming under his attention, Haley hiked her dress up farther.

He withdrew his hand from her and grabbed the light silk in his fists. It tore in his grip, and his heart stopped at the sound. With shuddering fingers, he shredded the dress. Raden would never get close enough to touch her again. His hands roamed along her exposed stomach, caressing her branded skin. "You're so perfect, Haley."

She gripped his shoulders and slid on top of him, completely naked, and pressed her bare sex against his lap. "I missed your cock so much."

Breathless, he laid her down on the seat and yanked open his belt and zipper, then pulled his cock out of his boxers.

"I'm dying to get inside you." Damian grazed her clit with his sensitive tip, and she jolted. He let out a deep growl as his cock found its way inside her smooth flesh. "Don't worry." He drove in as deep as he could. "I won't let them hurt you."

She licked along his throat. Her breath on his skin drove him insane. "Promise?"

"I promise." He pumped into her with a grunt as chills flooded his entire body. "I'm gonna take care of you, baby."

Haley whimpered beneath him, and he thrust a little harder, jerking her with his motions.

She stared up at him with dazed, half-closed eyes. "Did you miss fucking me?"

"You have no idea." He gave her a rough kiss, biting her plump bottom lip, losing coherence as she clenched around his dick.

She teased his lips with her tongue. "You missed my pussy?"

"Yes." Grunting, he forced himself to hold out for her climax, but his was relentless, rising to the surface. He fought the desperate urge. "You know I love your sweet little pussy, Haley."

"You feel so good, Damian." She breathed the words as he sank inside, filling her deeply.

"Fuck, I love you so much." He buried his face against her shoulder, intense heat swirling in his lower abdomen, rolling through his strained cock. "Tell me you're never gonna leave me."

"Never."

"Promise me." He slid in and out of her soft pussy with long strokes.

She nodded with a sharp breath. "I need to come." She dragged her nails under his collar, and he kept his steady pace, ready to explode.

Haley tugged on his loose tie. "Please let me come, Damian."

Breathing hard, he skimmed his tongue along her throat.

She tensed beneath him. "Please, it feels so good."

"You need me to let you come?"

Her moan sounded pained. "I'm so ready."

He ignored the agony in his bursting cock, grazing his teeth along her ear, and she gasped. With a smile, he trailed his fingers down her front and rubbed her clit while he glided his rigid length into her. "Come for me, angel."

"I'm coming." She tightened her legs around him as she pulled his shirt upward and raked her nails along his six-pack.

Every muscle in his body tensed. His cock almost hurt as his climax ripped through him, pouring his cum inside her in intense pulsing spasms. He groaned against her neck, pressing deeper into her as a powerful warmth rushed through his chest, and the shocking hot tears filled his eyes again.

As he descended from his extreme high, slowly regaining consciousness, his limbs felt numb. He rested on top of her, closing his eyes as her fingertips skated over his head. "I love you, Haley." He wasn't used to being so goddamn emotional, but he couldn't stop himself.

She let out a soft breath. "I love you more than anything, Damian."

He pulled back from her, and his throat tightened as he stared down into her deep-blue eyes. "You're the best thing that ever happened to me."

If he'd been given a second chance at this life with her, he wouldn't fuck it up again. It was time to declare war on his family.

* * *

Damian ambled down the hallway toward his bedroom. It was late afternoon, and he'd just spent eighteen hours at Adversus headquarters focused on attack strategies, working on assembling forces to take down his uncle. He had stopped going on missions, and his work hours had actually shortened since his promotion a few months earlier, but the new job somehow drained him.

He removed his tie and took off his wrinkled button-down shirt.

Emily squeaked. Her hands flew to her naked breasts as she turned her back to him. Haley rushed in front of him, wearing only a lacy bra and underwear.

"Hi." She smiled and pressed her palms to his bare chest, pushing him backward. "We're almost done here, sorry."

"What the fuck? Where the fuck are your clothes?"

Haley kept shoving him toward the doorway as Emily dressed in the distance. "We just went shopping. We're trying stuff on."

He drew his brows together. "Why?"

She sighed. "Because Emily has a date tonight. Get out of here."

"No, no, I'm all set. I'll leave." Emily collected a few scattered paper shopping bags. Her face blazed crimson as she hurried past him. "Thanks for everything, Haley."

Haley scrunched her nose. "Sorry, Em… Have fun tonight."

"I hope so." Emily glanced back with a smile, continuing down the hall. "I'll call you tomorrow."

Damian crossed the room and collapsed onto their bed with a groan.

Haley sat beside him a moment later, sliding a brush through her long hair. "She is terrified of you."

He pulled a pillow closer. He was nothing compared to that girl's mother.

Haley leaned across his back and set the brush on the nightstand. Her bare tits grazed his skin, and his cock stirred. He tilted his face toward her. She'd taken off all her clothes.

She traced the outline of the tattooed snake on his back, and he melted under her touch.

"Damian?" Her soft voice was almost a whisper, lulling him to sleep. "Do you know when we're going to attack Raden?"

His senses sharpened at the subject, and he turned, rolling onto his back. "Should be within a few weeks." He played with the ends of her long curls hanging over her breasts. "Maybe less. And you're not attacking anything, angel. You'll be safe here at home, understand?"

"Yes."

"Good." He propped himself up on his elbow. "I gotta go back to work, baby. I'm just here to pick up a few things."

She pulled her knees to her chest. "Okay."

Her position left her pretty sex exposed, drawing his gaze.

"I'm sorry." His voice came out grainy. "I want to stay."

"I know." She looked down. "Your job's important."

"Yeah." Damian couldn't stop staring between her thighs. He felt like toying with her for a few hours before allowing her to finish. "No, I think I'll spend a little time with you. Come here."

"What about work?" She crawled toward him.

"Don't worry about that. Come sit on my face."

With a little gasp, Haley did as she was told. She perched on top of his chest and settled her clit against his mouth.

Damian nuzzled his face against her sweet flesh. He was in for a long night.

Just after 2:00 AM, footsteps approached his office. Adam's frantic thoughts blared out in the hall. Damian straightened in his chair. This couldn't be good.

"Hey." Out of breath, Adam shut the door. "I just got a report from the clairvoyants."

"What happened?" Damian stood up. "Is Haley alright?"

"Yeah, she's fine. She's at your house." He ruffled his trimmed brown hair and smoothed it. "It's Emily. She was kidnapped about an hour ago. Cassie, too, but she was taken a few days ago. I don't think anyone knew she was missing until now."

"Who took them?"

"I don't know. My aunt Collette is headed here now." Adam shook his head. "Man, she was pissed when Emily decided to move up here. She is fucking... She's livid about this."

Damian crossed his arms over his chest. He had no desire to see Collette ever again. "Emily had a date tonight, right?"

"Yeah, that guy's dead." Adam adjusted his tie, pulling it loose. "She was living in the Hawthorne office building temporarily. That's where they snatched her." He stared at the floor. "Fuck, it feels like Haley all over again."

"Cameras?"

"None. And no witnesses. They slaughtered every man on the security team."

Damian raised his eyebrows. He'd personally chosen those men. "How'd they die?"

"Gruesome." Adam paused for a moment. "Reminds me of my parents' murders." He took a deep breath. "Could be bloodlings."

"Raden."

"That's what it looks like. Want to check it out?"

Damian nodded and grabbed his jacket.

The office building was littered with bodies. They had all been good men, they didn't deserve to die like that. They'd been practically shredded. And these men were incredible fighters, combat trained. Adam's bloodling theory seemed to hold up. A pack of bloodthirsty men could have left wounds like that. More animals than men, really, and Raden controlled a particularly evil bloodling pack. The same one he'd sent after Haley's mother.

They scanned the entire building. Haley's office called to his senses as he passed, but he shook it off. Jesus, that woman had a powerful hold on him.

He'd been awake for well over twenty-four hours, and his bed was calling to him. But Haley wouldn't be sleeping. She had most likely already heard about her cousins and needed him for support.

Her office door had been left slightly open, and the lights were off inside. As far as he knew, the bloodlings hadn't been after Haley, they wouldn't have any reason to go in there. Her essence emanated from behind the door, beckoning to him, and he hesitated by the elevator. He might as well take a look.

He flicked the light switch, and a lamp on her desk emitted a yellow glow. A figure wearing a black dress sat in an armchair in the shadowy corner.

Damian halted, and the door slammed behind him.

"I caught you."

Her singing taunts had echoed through his mind for years. Shimmering green spun through a black cloud as she conjured her powers. It snaked around his body and forced him against the door.

"She won't protect you this time."

As she stepped closer, Marybelle's face came into view. One side was badly scarred from her encounter with Haley. The burn covered her skin in the shape of a small handprint. Damian smirked.

The feathery smoke tightened around his throat, and Marybelle grasped his belt in her fingers. *Ugh, fuck... Sadistic fucking cunt.*

"It's been so long, my pet."

He swallowed. "She'll find me."

Marybelle nodded. "Yes, she will. And then I get to kill your little queen bitch." She smiled. "I'll slice her up and feed her to you."

A darkness inside him surfaced, and his voice dropped to a growl. "You won't touch her."

She giggled. "Oh, you are going to get it."

Damian tried to resist, but she drove him forward with her powers. His heart raced as she bent him over Haley's desk.

His cell phone vibrated in his pocket, and she didn't seem to notice.

Marybelle leaned in close to him, sliding her tongue along his throat. "Mmm, I miss the way you taste."

Damian clutched the desk, preparing for her assault.

She gave an exaggerated sigh. "Who. Keeps. Calling?" She snatched his phone from his pocket. "Oh. Of course."

Marybelle tossed it on the desk, and Haley's picture displayed on the screen.

"Okay, little pet. I'll let you answer it."

Damian tensed as she opened his pants and jerked them down his legs along with his boxers. Her lips lingered beside his ear.

"Go ahead, answer the phone."

He closed his eyes. *Fuck no.* Haley couldn't know about this. He was supposed to be her protector, not some weak fucker pinned down across her desk.

She sliced her razor-sharp nails across his naked backside and spoke through clenched teeth. "Fine, I'll answer it."

"No." The word flew out of his mouth, and he was instantly sorry. He shouldn't have broken so easily.

She paused briefly. "It seems you have a new weakness."

Listless, she walked around and plopped down into Haley's chair. "I don't really care for it to be perfectly honest."

As his pulse slowed, Damian rested his face against the wood.

"That little bitch must rock your world." Marybelle picked up his phone and tapped the screen. "Oh, she texted you. How cute." She cocked an eyebrow. "And she calls you baby. That's very original."

She threw the phone to the floor and leaned back in the chair.

"Raden says she weakens you."

He snorted. His muscles tightened as he worked to stand upright, but the dark clouds held him still.

Marybelle ran a finger along the scar on her cheek. "I think you are the one who makes her weak. She's more powerful than any of us. Our *queen*. And yet she will never embrace her true purpose. She denies her powers. Because of you."

His stomach tensed as the reality of her words set in.

He froze as she advanced toward him. His mind raced with memories of her sick painful games, but somehow the hollow, consuming ache she'd stirred inside him hurt worse than any of her usual devices.

Leaning toward him, she clasped his chin and forced him to face her.

"The queen witch should be with someone a little stronger than *you*, don't you think?"

His labored breath caught in his chest.

Releasing him, she stood, and the smoke dissipated. "I'm bored with you."

Free from the suffocating hold, Damian straightened. The cursed tears threatened to surface, and he cleared his ragged throat, lifting his pants and buttoning them. The crazy bitch had vanished, leaving him alone with his thoughts. He didn't want to admit that her words had affected him, but he couldn't seem to take a full breath. His heart felt shattered in his chest.

He grabbed his phone from the floor, then got the fuck out of there.

Haley called again when he was on his way back to headquarters, but he wasn't in any condition to talk. Marybelle was involved with Emily's kidnapping, an adversary he couldn't hunt down. He would keep his focus on the monster he could attack.

CHAPTER EIGHTEEN

Haley tightened the belt around her long black jacket once more as she walked toward Damian's office. He'd been acting distant for several days, agitated beyond belief.

Trying to hide her frown, she tapped her knuckles on the door.

"Come in."

Damian glanced up when she stepped inside and dropped his gaze back to his desk.

Haley paused at his reaction, then softly clicked the door shut. The blinds were closed behind him. "It's so dark in here."

He set down his papers as she approached him.

She eased onto the edge of his desk. "Did you hear that Adam found Emily and Cassie last night?"

He nodded, distracted, and shifted his attention back to his work.

She let the silence sink in for a moment. The sleeves of his dress shirt were rolled up, and she caressed the black tattoos on his forearm. He hardly acknowledged her presence, still studying the papers.

"Well…" Adrenaline pumped through her as she licked her lips and untied her belt. The lapels fell open, and she trailed her fingers down her breasts, bare under the jacket. "I just wanted to see you."

Damian pushed his chair back, running his palm down his face. "This is my goddamn office, Haley." He gestured between her legs. "You've been walking around headquarters like that?"

"No, I was…covered." She couldn't take his intense glare and wrenched the coat around herself. She fell silent for a moment. This wasn't like him at all, something wasn't right.

"Have you been sleeping?" Her voice came out weak.

"A little." He didn't make eye contact with her as he nodded at the couch against the wall, his new bed.

Tears welled up inside her, overwhelming her, but she forced her emotions to settle.

"You've fucked me in my office before." She spoke in a quiet voice. "I don't see why yours is different."

Something snapped behind his gaze, and Damian pointed toward the door. "I'm working on something here. You need to leave."

"What?" Gaping at him, she couldn't move. His thoughts seemed closed off, shadowed by blinding anger.

"Stay the fuck out of my head, Haley."

She tensed up, and the tears she'd held back rose to her eyes, blurring her vision. "Is it…because of Marybelle?"

With a deep growl, he lowered his head and dragged his hands along his scalp. "If you already knew, why did you ask?"

The pure venom in his voice stabbed into her, and Haley clutched her chest. "What do you mean?"

"You thought if you played naïve long enough, I'd tell you what she did?" He buried his face in his hands. "Fuck."

Chills ran under her skin. Her voice came out cold and shaky. "What did she do?"

Damian looked up at her, leaning on his elbows. "You said you knew?"

Murderous thoughts raced through her mind, and she forced herself to breathe. "What happened?"

He shook his head. "Nothing."

His dark expression tugged at her heart. *Stay calm, just relax.* Whatever it was could remain hidden.

Reaching forward with a jittering hand, she touched her fingertips to his face, grazing his overgrown facial hair. "It's okay if you don't want to tell me."

Damian shifted in his chair, leaning away from her touch, and stared down at his hands in his lap. "She got into my head." He rolled his shoulders as he leaned back. "About us."

Panic flickered through her chest. Her limbs started tremoring, and she held her arms across her waist. "Our love is too strong for her to break." Holding back tears, she met his gaze, feeling suddenly fragile and exposed. "Right?"

He hesitated for a torturous second, then moved his hands to her knees and nodded. His warm palms soothed her vibrating nerves, and she took a long breath.

Damian sighed as his muscles loosened. "I've been a prick."

She shook her head, her heart overflowing with tenderness. "I should have come to you sooner." She wiped her fingers under her eyes. "I knew something was different with us."

"It's not your fault." His hands crept under her coat. "You deserve so much fucking better than me."

Haley drifted her arms around his neck. "She really did climb into your head, didn't she," she mumbled.

Grasping her naked hips, Damian dropped his gaze with a trace of a smile. "She has your handprint on her face."

She caught her bottom lip between her teeth. His handsome expression melted her. "Well, she *had* it…" She rolled her eyes. "Now she doesn't really have a face."

He pulled his brows together. "What did you say?"

"You know, because…" She faltered. "Emily killed her yesterday. I thought… You didn't know that?"

His gaze wandered over her lap. "I heard they were rescued… I haven't read the file yet." He palmed his jawline. "Is she really fucking dead?"

"Yes." A smile broke across her lips. "Emily destroyed her."

Thoughtful, Damian glanced downward. After a moment, he cleared his throat. His neck muscles were tensed, and his Adam's apple moved as he swallowed.

Her heart ached for him, and she pulled him closer. He wrapped his arms around her, enfolding her with raw power, and pressed his face between her breasts.

Haley rested her lips on his head. "She won't ever hurt you again."

He tightened his grip on her, and she relaxed in his suffocating hold, overcome with a fierce urge to protect him, grateful the vile witch was dead.

Damian clung to her for a minute longer before he let go.

Settling his gaze on her chest, he opened her jacket, then kissed along her breast and nudged his nose against her nipple. "You still love me? Even though I fucking bailed on you this week?"

She gave him a gentle look. "I'm crazy in love with you."

He sat back, lifting the corner of his mouth, and drifted his gaze up to hers. "You been sleeping okay without me there?"

She shrugged a shoulder. Frenzied thoughts had plagued her mind since her cousins had been abducted. Sleep hadn't been much of a priority.

He looked away from her. "I should have come home."

"You were going through something too."

He folded his arms over his chest and glared at the desk. "I've been focused. We're taking down Raden and his army by the end of next week."

Mention of Raden always sent a cold shock of fear through her. With a deep breath, she set her emotions aside, her man had made it his personal mission to keep her safe.

"What about Lucifer?"

He took her hand and glided his thumb over each of her glossy nails. "He's next. After I murder Raden."

His absent tone seemed slightly forced, and Haley closed her fingers around his. "Are you sure you want to kill your father?"

Damian shook his head. "He hasn't left me a choice. I can't let him live if he's gonna hurt you."

She lifted his hand and held it to her chest. Lowering her face, she kissed his rough knuckles. "You're a good man, Damian."

"No." He pulled his hand away and dropped it in his lap. "I'm not." His mind flashed a shadowy glimpse of Marybelle's scarred face, and he abruptly changed his course of thought.

A simmering wrath boiled inside her that she couldn't ignore. Breathing faster, she pursed her lips for a moment. "Did she touch you?"

He didn't answer, keeping his gaze trained on his desk with a stone expression.

His silence stabbed into her, and Haley bit down hard on her lower lip. "Never mind." She shook her head, battling the storm of emotions raging inside her. "I shouldn't have asked."

Damian stood up, and she raised her gaze as he towered over her. He slipped his fingers into her hair and slid them down through the long waves. "She didn't make me fuck her or anything… I just feel like shit about it cause I hate being a helpless motherfucker."

She wiped away the tear falling down her cheek and hopped off the desk. Gripping his solid chest with her palms, she nestled her forehead against his neck, swallowing past the lump in her throat.

With a delicate touch, he brushed his fingertips down her back. "Haley…" He let out a slow breath. "You know how powerful you are, right?"

She didn't reply, unsure where his question was leading.

He continued. "You know I don't control you outside of the bedroom. Or…maybe I do… I'm too fucking possessive, I know that." Drawing back from her, he tilted her chin upward.

She gazed up at his vulnerable expression. He looked exhausted, broken down. His eyes reflected pure hurt. *Marybelle.*

"You're so fucking strong, Haley." He furrowed his brows. "You're capable of anything. Don't let me get in your way, okay? Don't let me hold you back anymore."

"Damian."

"You can do anything, Haley. You're the fucking queen, why would you be with me?"

Her heartbeat sped up. *So that's what she said to you.* Forcing her breath to calm, she fought the angry tears brimming below the surface and held her focus on his tie, trailing her fingers down along the silk. "I know I'm a strong, independent woman, Damian… But I still need you by my side." Lifting her gaze to his, she reached up and brushed her palm along his beard. "You're a warrior."

He stood stone-still, holding her gaze. His eyes clouded with emotion, and her heart broke in her chest.

Choking back tears, she stood on her toes and leaned toward his ear. "I'm so lucky to be with you."

Damian grunted. His muscles flexed as he squeezed his arms around her, increasing his grip until she could hardly breathe. She relished the feeling, resting in his arms while he held her, and her anxieties dissolved away.

He groaned deeply. "I should have known you'd make me feel whole again."

Haley closed her eyes, bathed in dreamy emotions. "Are you coming home to me tonight?"

"Yes."

Her heart beat faster at his response. "Can you leave now?"

Damian loosened his hold and pulled back from her. "I still gotta take care of a few things. Won't take more than a couple hours, though."

She pulled in the corner of her mouth with a nod.

He studied her features. "I'm sorry, angel."

"I understand." Haley looked down and cinched her belt.

"I know I was an asshole about your jacket." He played with the strip of black fabric tied around her waist. "I don't like that you're wearing this in public."

She flitted her gaze toward his. "What's wrong with it?"

"Fuck-me heels and a coat." He sat down in his chair. "You gave a hard-on to every guy you passed in this fucking place."

She giggled. "You're the only one who knows I'm not wearing anything under it."

He picked up his papers from the desk, silent.

Haley watched him for a moment. He'd never turned her down before, and it stung, but it seemed as if he needed time to get his head straight after encountering the dark witch. "I'll see you at home."

Damian paused his work and jerked her lapels closed. He fastened each button and tugged her belt tighter. "Go directly to your car."

"Seriously?"

"The guys around here are desperate, chauvinist dicks."

"Okay, baby." She smiled and leaned forward. "I love you." She'd meant to just give him a light kiss, but his lips felt so good. Opening her lips, she ventured into his mouth with her tongue and instantly ran wet between her legs. With a little groan, she backed off.

"I love you too." His voice had gone soft, and it sent a thrill of confidence through her.

She missed his kinky games. Her thighs clenched together on their own as she straightened. "Hurry home."

He nodded. "Drive safe."

Oversexed and frustrated, Haley headed for the door. Fucking Marybelle was still antagonizing her from the grave.

As she neared the elevator, a familiar voice shouted around the corner.

"This is ridiculous." Emily threw her hands up and walked away from the guard's desk, her light-blue eyes glistening with tears.

When Emily approached her, Haley touched her arm. "Hey, what's going on?"

She sniffled. "They just took him away. It's like Guantanamo in here."

"Took who away?"

Emily looked toward the elevator beside them. "He isn't a monster." She pulled her dark-red locks over her shoulder. "He doesn't belong in there."

"You're talking about…the bloodling who kidnapped you?"

With a downward gaze, Emily shrugged her shoulder. "I know how it looks, but he isn't like his family." She cleared the tears from her cheeks. "I can't just leave him there. They won't even let me talk to him."

Hopefully she wasn't suffering from Stockholm syndrome, but her cousin was a smart woman, and Haley had her own experience with a seductive captor.

"Where is he exactly?"

"The prison cells. But the elevator won't let you go down there unless you have clearance."

"What about the stairs?"

Emily's gaze drifted toward the stairwell door. "I'm sure it's guarded."

"Let's give it a try."

"Really?" Emily clasped her chest. "Thank you, Haley. I just need to make sure he's okay."

When they reached the bottom of the staircase, they approached a metal door labeled Restricted Area. The guard's station beside it appeared empty. A security camera hovered in the corner of the ceiling.

Emily peered into a dark office behind the desk. "There's no one here." With a shaking hand, she tried the door handle, but it didn't budge. She tapped the scanner built into the wall. "We need an ID badge."

Haley checked her surroundings and breezed around the desk. Rifling through the drawers, she snagged a set of keys with a thick white card attached. Her heart pounded in her chest as she pressed the card to the scanner.

The door buzzed, and heavy bolts rattled along the seam. Emily flashed her a wide-eyed look and wrenched the giant door open.

Haley followed her through and closed the door. The locks slid back into place, and she held tightly to the keys. With unsure steps, they proceeded down the dark hall, illuminated by a single yellow light bulb at one end.

As they rounded a corner, shrieking voices grew louder. Thick steel doors lined the walls.

"It's hard to focus on him with all these others around." Emily jolted as a growling voice blared a high-pitched sound behind a nearby door. "What are they doing to them?"

Though Haley tried to silence them, the prisoners' energy penetrated her mind, a jumble of emotions brought on by excruciating pain. Screams echoed all around, and she held her arms around herself as she walked. "Let's keep moving."

Farther into the dungeon, the sparse lighting flickered.

"He's close," Emily whispered. "I can feel him." She changed course and headed down a cement staircase.

"Hey!" A man in a guard's uniform jogged in her direction and Haley slipped the keys into her pocket.

"Ma'am, this is a restricted area."

"Oh." She moved away from the staircase as Emily disappeared into the shadows. "Yes, I know. I'm Adam Hawthorne's sister. He asked me to come down here."

"Nice try, kitten. Let's go." He caught her arm and yanked her beside him.

Shit, shit, shit… She couldn't abandon Emily in that horrible place.

"I'm supposed to be here." Haley made eye contact with him. "My name is Haley Hawthorne. Adam wanted me to check on one of the prisoners."

He scowled. "You want me to call him and check out that story of yours?"

"Um…"

"That's what I thought." He glanced from her breasts to her face. "How about if you let me see those tits, I can forget you were here."

She stood openmouthed for a beat. "Um, okay."

"Yeah?" He fingered her collar, shifting closer to her. "Let's see 'em."

"Mmhm." She tried to think of a way out.

"Come on, what you got under this?"

"Donaldson."

Haley flinched at the male voice. The guard holding her looked toward the other man, and she inched backward.

The other guard approached, focused on his blood-soaked hands as he wiped them with a dirty rag. "Pierce wants a shift change. I'm heading upstairs to take over for Nichols. Why aren't you at your post?"

She sneaked around the corner and rushed down the cement stairs.

"What the fuck? Where'd she go?" Donaldson shouted.

Slipping off her heels, she dashed to the other side of the corridor and ducked into the shadows. Beyond the tormented screams, she singled out Emily's thoughts. She was in a solitary cell at the end of a long hall, speaking to a prisoner.

"I'm calling the fuckin' boss, bitch," the guard hollered. "We'll find your ass."

As he moseyed closer, she backed against the cold wall, hidden in the dark. Something wet grazed across her hand, and she jerked away.

"I don't know, sir, she said her name was Haley Hawthorne." The guard was on his phone. "That girl was all over me. Even offered to flash me her titties so I wouldn't call you."

Oh, come on. Her brother didn't need to hear that. Adam would be pissed at her, but at least they had accomplished what they'd gone there to do.

The guard wandered down a separate hallway, and she held her stomach, sick from the rush of adrenaline. She drifted sideways along the wall and slippery fingers closed around her wrist. Covering her shriek, she stumbled away.

She squinted toward the darkness, and someone stared back at her with wild eyes. Iron shackles held his wrists and ankles against the wall and streaks of blood ran down his emaciated body.

Haley rubbed her jittering hand on her jacket and the starved man's blood smeared across her skin. She crept deeper into the hall, holding her shoes with a white-knuckle grip.

Blocking out the awful noises, Haley focused on her cousin's energy and headed toward it. She opened the solid metal door at the end of the corridor. A man, stripped naked, stood in front of Emily, his wrists bound by chains that hung from the ceiling. Fresh bruises and welts covered his scarred body.

Haley slid her shoes onto her feet. "Emily? Sorry, we have to go."

Emily gave a little nod. Quivering, she swayed toward the doorway with a vacant expression.

Haley gently clasped her shoulder and led her out of the cell and down the dark passageway.

"Get on the ground!" The perverted guard clenched a nightstick in his hand and pointed it in their direction as he advanced.

The other guard joined him an instant later. "Jesus, Donaldson, there's two of them."

"Shut up, I left the desk for one goddamn minute." He glowered at Haley. "I said get on your fucking knees!"

Emily began to lower herself to the floor, and Haley seized her wrist.

"He told me to show him my tits earlier, I don't think we should get on our knees."

"He's gonna beat us to death with that thing."

The guard clamped onto Haley's shoulder and worked to shove her down.

Emily jumped forward and grabbed his collar. Golden light burst from her hands as she pushed him, and he wobbled backward.

His confused look turned to violent rage, and he raised the baton.

The other guard rushed in front of him. "Boss is here."

Damian walked up to them, and Haley's heart lurched in her chest.

"This one has powers, sir." The guard jutted his finger toward Emily. "That must be how they got in here."

"Get back to work."

With a nod, the guard proceeded down the hall, and the other followed him.

Emily stepped back and gripped Haley's arm. "She was helping me."

Silent, Damian kept his jaw firmly shut.

Emily shrank behind her. "It's my fault."

Haley touched Emily's fingers around her arm. "I thought that guard was on the phone with Adam."

Damian narrowed his eyes, lit with intensity. "Adam's in the medical wing because he was bitten by a prisoner." He gestured down the hall toward the cell they'd just emerged from. "*That* prisoner."

Emily lowered her forehead to Haley's shoulder. "Is Adam okay?"

Crossing his arms, Damian nodded and glared at Haley.

"Emily needed me."

"We'll talk about it at home."

His sharp tone sent a shiver through her. She drifted after him as he headed toward the exit. Emily let go of her arm and walked beside her, clutching her hands together.

They walked by the steel torture chambers, and Haley darted her gaze away from the splattered blood on the cement floor. A desperate scream tore through the air, rattling her core.

"Why are they torturing them?"

Damian didn't answer and turned down the quieter hallway.

She hurried forward and groped his abdomen, tugging on his shirt. "Why are they doing that?"

"Not your concern, Haley." Damian pulled his keys from his pocket as they approached the door. "How did you get in here?"

She handed him the stolen keys. "Is it for information? Don't you have mind readers?"

He halted and gritted his teeth. "They're monsters."

"They have feelings."

A hint of a smile lingered on his lips, and he scanned his card over the panel. "These ones are immune to mind readers." He dropped the keys onto the guard's desk as he passed.

Donaldson looked up. "Thank you, sir."

Haley huddled closer to Damian, keeping pace with him. "And what about Emily's man? Did you give him that beating?"

"Not me personally." He looked down at her. "He attacked your brother."

"I know." The man's beaten body haunted her thoughts, and she tried to shrug it off. "It feels wrong."

"That's why you're not allowed in there." Damian veered her toward the elevator and pressed a code into the control panel. "Did she drive here?"

Emily glanced up. "Uh, I did, yes."

Haley withdrew from Damian. Her cousin didn't look quite as anguished as before, but pain still shadowed her gaze. "Are you gonna be okay?"

Emily turned toward the doors, waiting for them to open. "I'm fine." Her voice quieted to a whisper. "Sorry I got you in trouble."

"It's okay." Haley followed her into the elevator. "He's not gonna beat me." She smiled.

Damian snorted. The muscles in his tattooed forearms tensed as he shoved his hands in his pockets. *"You're getting punished tonight."*

Sensation rushed between her thighs. *Oh God...* She shifted her stance, aching for his touch.

Haley grasped her fluttering stomach and turned her attention to Emily. "Should you be driving? Why don't I give you a ride?"

"No. I need to drive." Emily closed her eyes and wiped her palm across her tear-stained cheek. "I just want to be alone."

The doors parted at the parking garage.

Haley gave her a tender look. "Be sure to call if you need anything."

"I will." Emily squeezed Haley's arm. "Thanks." She held onto her chest as she walked out of the elevator.

Haley gripped her elbows with a weighted sigh and started toward her car. "Did you see her face?"

Damian strolled alongside her. "Doesn't excuse what you did."

Her lips parted at his gravelly voice, and she fidgeted with the ends of her hair. "She just wanted to talk to him."

"That place is locked down for a reason, Haley. You should have come to me."

"Well—"

"It's fucking dangerous."

She drew in the corners of her mouth, stopping when she got to the driver's side of her car. "You're right. I'm sorry."

Damian watched in silence as she fumbled with her keys. He reached forward and ran his finger along the dried blood on her hand. "Are you hurt?"

"It's not my blood." Her soft voice shook a little.

He nodded with a long sigh and folded his arms around her. "I'll see what I can do about your cousin's man."

Haley buried her face against his hard chest and breathed in his warm, masculine scent. "Thank you."

He stroked his fingers through her hair. "I'll be home in an hour."

CHAPTER NINETEEN

Haley had started baking after her shower, attempting to clear her head of the awful Adversus dungeon, but the snickerdoodles weren't enough to set her mind at ease.

An engine rumbled in the garage and her pulse spiked. She cleared a bit of flour dust from her thigh and adjusted the apron strap along her neck.

Barefoot, she had settled on a new black bra and panties set, transparent with pretty designs in the fabric, and just tied her ruffled apron over the lingerie.

Damian strode in from the hallway. He looked her over as he picked up a cookie. "Trying to get on my good side?"

With a little smirk, she swiveled toward the counter behind her and stirred a bowl of white frosting. Her panties left the bottom half of her ass exposed, and Damian took in the view.

She bent a little more than necessary and retrieved a baking sheet full of sugar cookies from the oven.

He took a jagged breath. "You're in trouble, sweet girl."

Tingles surged through her clit, and Haley sucked some frosting off her finger, slinking against the counter.

Damian pulled off his tie. "I released your cousin's man. In case you were wondering." He ran his thumb across her chin. "You have a little flour here…"

A smile broke across her face, and she held her hands behind her back, stifling the urge to jump on him.

He took hold of her hips and turned her around. She braced her palms against the counter as he dragged his calloused fingers down her back.

"Donaldson said you offered to flash him." He spread a little dab of frosting on her ass and knelt down.

Her jaw went slack as he closed his mouth over her flesh with a biting grasp. "Did you?" He licked and sucked her skin, then his lips traveled to her inner thigh, and he wrenched her panties aside.

His tongue drifted along her clit, and she pressed her fingernails into the marble.

"Yes." She sucked in a breath as he bared his teeth against her pussy. "Or… I didn't mean…"

Damian stood to full height and snatched a wooden spoon from the drawer. He tugged on her panties. "Take these off."

Her vision clouded as she shimmied them down her legs. He turned her and his powerful arm swept in front of her.

She leaned forward as he pressed his erection into her hip.

"Bad girl, Haley." He kissed her neck with an open mouth and the wooden spoon pressed against the back of her thighs as his fingers explored between them.

He grabbed her breast, pinching her nipple through the sheer bra. "You know who these belong to."

Her breath came in short bursts, and she rubbed her ass against his hand, anticipating her spanking.

"I know you want it, baby." Damian caught her ear between his teeth, and she gasped, lightheaded.

He swatted her with the spoon, and she bent forward, leaning across his forearm as he held her. He struck her again, harder and harder until the smacks started to sting. She moaned, parting her legs a little, and he stopped.

Damian tossed the spoon into the sink and turned her to face him. He grabbed her sensitive backside. "You learn your lesson, angel?"

She licked her lips, dazed, and shook her head.

He opened his belt with a half-smile. "Good." He held her gaze as he dropped his zipper. "Strip."

Haley untied the apron and slipped it over her head in a languid motion. She unhooked the front clasp of her bra and let the straps slide off her shoulders.

Damian studied her naked body as he pulled out his cock. He reached into the bowl of frosting and smeared a little onto his tip.

"Lick it off."

She dropped to her knees and flicked her tongue along the wet slit in the head of his cock. Damian latched onto her ponytail, watching her as she lapped at his stiff flesh with hungry licks.

Haley glanced up at him from under her dark lashes and fondled his testicles with her hands as she sucked him clean. He plunged his fingers into her hair, sliding off her hair-tie, and gripped her wavy curls in his fists.

"Come here." His voice sounded thick as he withdrew his cock from her lips.

She stood, and Damian grabbed her thighs with strong hands, then sat her on top of the counter.

"Let me see your pussy."

Haley reached down and spread herself open for him. He knelt in front of her and touched his tongue to her fingers, barely grazing her exposed sex. Writhing on the counter, she pointed toward her aching clit. He ignored her and instead licked along her inner thigh.

"Please." She cradled his face in her hands. "I need your mouth on me."

He stared up at her for a moment, then leaned forward and kissed between her legs. Slow at first, he used only his soft lips. His scratchy facial hair tickled her sensitive pussy.

Her heartbeat pounded as he trailed his tongue between her slit.

Damian moaned against her, biting gently. "You taste so fucking good, Haley."

He rose and looked down at his swollen dick, turning almost purple at the tip, gleaming in his palm.

Haley swept her thumb over his lips, wet with her juices. She couldn't resist kissing him and ran her tongue along his moist beard.

Damian forced himself into her with a groan. "Sexy witch."

Sighing as her vision went blurry, she rode his steady strokes. "I've been craving you."

His growl rumbled against her throat, sending ripples of pleasure through her as he played with her breasts. He closed his mouth over her shoulder and bit into her tender skin.

Haley gasped. "Wait, I'm posing for wedding photos tomorrow." She shied away from his fierce teeth. "No bite marks, it's a strapless dress."

He paused with his dick buried between her legs. "Strapless… Why are you in the photos?"

The waves of desire were too much to bear, and she wriggled toward him. "Cause I'm in the wedding."

"Are you wearing the white dress?"

Haley swayed her hips forward and back on his sublimely hard cock while he remained annoyingly still. "No, baby, that's what the bride wears." She unfastened his buttons and jerked his shirt off him. "I have my own dress. It's blue."

His chest and shoulders tensed, and he went a little deeper. The hunger in her lower belly demanded attention, and she clenched around his pulsing shaft.

Still unmoving, he leaned in, taking her throat between his lips, careful not to leave marks. "The bride is the only one who wears the white dress?"

Her body shivered as her need continued to go unfulfilled. "Yes."

Damian licked and kissed her neck, sending her into madness. She grabbed his backside, sinking her nails into the muscles, and he only pressed harder inside her.

She swallowed her desperate desire. "The bride also wears a veil, usually."

He finally withdrew and plunged in deep with a delicious thrust. "Do you think you'll wear a veil?"

Opening her eyes, she rested against his rigid shoulder as he filled her again and again.

"If I was the bride?" Time stood still as she awaited his reply.

Damian's cock hardened further, enormous and sliding along her clitoris. He skimmed his tongue across her ear, and her gnawing ache increased, growing painful.

"Yeah."

Her shuddering breath caught in her throat and her legs lost feeling. The unquenched desire mingled with a fluttering warmth inside her. "Probably."

He kept up his torment, jerking in and out, and Haley reached her peak, moaning as she released with a pleasured rush around his steadily pounding cock. Chills spread across her skin as his words sank in. She suppressed the euphoric urge to start weeping.

"I didn't say you could come, beautiful girl." Damian picked her up and brought her down to the floor. "On your knees." He gripped his slippery dick. Dark purplish-red and huge, it looked ready to burst. "Play with your tits for me. Hold them out."

Haley widened her knees at his feet and groped her breasts. She lifted and squeezed them around his tip as he touched himself.

"Ugh, fuck you're sexy." Damian stopped stroking, and hot liquid poured in spasms onto her naked breasts. He dragged the head of his cock across her nipple. *"Mine."* His deep voice resounded through the corners of her mind.

A smile played across her lips as he shoved his spent cock back into his pants. Reaching up, she snagged a towel from the counter.

Damian sat down on the floor beside her and leaned against the cabinet. "Such a hurry to clean up." He relaxed his muscles, resting his head back, and gazed at her breasts, covered with his cum. "That's how I claim you."

A little giggle escaped her throat as she wiped the terrycloth over her chest. Her heart nagged her to ask about his earlier wedding comment. He wasn't the type to say things he didn't mean, even while he was getting off. Then again, her memory was a little fuzzy on his exact words. She'd most likely read too much into it.

CHAPTER TWENTY

The conversation still puzzled her the next day, playing continually through her mind. He had halted completely, still insanely hard, but he'd held himself inside her. As if that part of the talk was important. Or he could have just been trying to drive her crazy with lust. He did love to tease her and treat her like his little sex toy.

She waited outside a mountain lodge hotel beside Ginger's red BMW convertible, shifting back and forth in her high heels. The dark-blue bridesmaid dress was tighter than when she'd had it fitted a few weeks earlier. Probably all the frosting and cookies she ate the night before. Not to mention her constant stress-eating while Emily and Cassie were missing.

Haley inched her dress down a little at her hips, and the hem floated just past her ankles. Damian wasn't exactly the kind of man who would get married. She could be content with that. Boyfriend had a nice ring to it. But the daydream of wearing his ring on her finger, being his actual wife, sent tingles through her.

"Excuse me, miss?" A man approached from across the parking lot. His light-brown hair was longer on top and shaved on the sides and back of his head. He raised a well-built arm and ran his fingers through it. "I've never been here. Do you know where the waterfalls are?"

She straightened, pointing behind him. "They're on the other side of the lodge over there, just follow that sidewalk."

He swiveled his head. "Just right over there?"

Haley stiffened as her intuition perked up. She flinched when he turned back to her.

"Oh, a little jumpy." He had a nice smile, but there was something off about him. His mind was blank except for a continuous humming sound. "Are you in a wedding today?"

"No. A wedding photo shoot, actually."

The lodge doors opened, and Ginger headed down the front stairs with a large white garment bag on her arm.

"Is this the bride?" He wiped his palms on his jeans.

Haley focused on his hands, her senses waking again. His thoughts revealed nothing, thick with chaotic energy.

"It's canceled. Noah isn't coming. Some work emergency." Ginger rolled her eyes. "Everything's an emergency there. Who's this?"

"I'm Sterling." He extended his hand. His green eyes sparkled with a golden hue.

"Hi." Ginger shook it briefly.

Stunned by his eyes for a moment, Haley blinked as she opened the passenger door. "Did you talk to Aimee?"

"Yeah, I told her to turn around." Ginger eyed Sterling on her way to the driver's side. She tossed her dress into the backseat and got in.

"See ya." Sterling gave a short nod.

Haley pulled on her seat belt with a hammering heartbeat.

Ginger shuffled through her purse for her keys. "I get that his work has to take priority sometimes, but it feels a little like I'm not important."

Sterling planted his hand on Haley's door and jumped into the backseat of the convertible. He jerked a fistful of Ginger's blond hair and wrapped a familiar collar around her neck. "Don't move, Your Majesty, or I will hurt her." He dangled an identical collar in front of Haley. "Be a good girl and put this on."

"Don't do it, Haley." Ginger slid her hand into her pocket. "Let him do what he's gonna do."

"False bravery doesn't last when the real pain starts." Sterling jutted the collar forward. "Trust that I will show her real pain, Haley."

"What happens if I put the collar on?"

"You don't get to ask questions." He tossed it onto Haley's lap and ripped Ginger's hand out of her pocket. "Every time you ask a question, I push a blade under one of her fingernails."

"Okay." Haley slipped the ethereal rope around her throat, and her magic disappeared. Powerless and chained once more, she craned her neck to face him as tears filled her eyes. "It's done."

"Good decision, sweetheart." Sterling stretched his arm between them, revealing a gold coin, etched with black markings, in his palm. He slid his thumb over the strange-looking drakpiece, and it glimmered with a shining light. "Both of you are going to hold onto me while we take a little trip."

"No." Ginger hopped up, working against his hold on her hair, and let out a piercing scream. "Somebody help!"

He wrestled her back into her seat, and Haley clawed at his eyes, aiming to gouge them out. With a roar, he opened his jaws and snapped at her fingers with rows of extending fangs. She shrieked and yanked her hand back. He grabbed her arm in a vice-like grip, and the transport coin came to life, surrounding them with glaring yellow light.

Haley and Ginger fell onto a black marble floor as Sterling released them.

"I expect you both to sit perfectly still." He stalked across the empty chamber and stood in front of the iron door, guarding it. "Or I'll make you do things to each other."

The air had gone stale and empty. He'd brought them to Hell. The square outline in Ginger's front pocket had to be her phone, she'd reached for it in the car. Haley clutched to the tiny hope that she'd successfully dialed someone.

"I thought you'd be more attractive." Sterling directed his steady glare at Haley. "The way Marybelle talked about you. Queen witch." He spat on the floor. "Emily is prettier."

He must belong to the bloodling pack who took Emily and Cassie. One of Raden's bloodthirsty minions.

"And blondie? Your fiancé is an Adversus soldier?"

Ginger kept her mouth in a straight line as she gripped her knees close to her chest.

"Yep, I bet he is scrambling. Raden only had one Hawthorne witch this morning. Now he's got three."

Haley's chin began to tremble. "What?"

"Was that a question?" He flipped open his blade. "What did I say about asking questions, bitch?"

She shook her head as tears flowed down her cheeks. "I'm sorry."

Sterling sneered. "I'll give you a pass. Just this once." He adjusted his belt and put his knife away. "While you were busy dressing up for your fucking photos, Emily was here. Being branded."

Ginger bent forward and laid her head on her arms. "Oh no." She drew in a breath. "Oh Jesus, not Emily too." She flashed a hateful look toward Sterling. "Fucking sick freaks—"

Sterling marched forward and hovered over her. He bared his sharpening teeth, and Ginger cowered lower. "Raden's gonna brand you too, little witch."

The door swung open, and a scaly creature beckoned from the doorway. "Raden wants them in his bedchamber."

Ginger broke into sobs, and the sound cut into Haley's heart as she rose from the cold floor.

"Di arak de'erden." Haley spoke the words clearly with as much authority as she could.

Sterling grinned. "Spells don't work with the collar on, sweetheart." He jabbed his knuckles into her back. "Move."

She shuffled forward, whispering the Trinnian command under her breath.

Sterling snaked his hand into her hair and brought his lips against hers with a light graze. "Shut up. Or I will bite your tongue off."

Haley tried to back away from his mouth, but he held her firmly.

"Now smile for me and say *yes, Sterling.*"

"Yes, Sterling." Haley gasped as he tugged her lower lip between his teeth.

He patted his fingers on her cheek. "That's a good girl."

His eyes carried a shocking power in them. The memory of Emily's beaten man in the Adversus dungeon crossed her mind. The chained bloodling's gaze had seethed with rage, a dark glitter of deep-green and gold.

She lifted her silk skirt at her thigh as she tried to keep pace behind Sterling. "I saw your brother. In the Adversus dungeons."

His muscles stiffened, and he stopped in his tracks.

"At least I think he was. You have the same eyes."

251

Sterling turned and crept toward her.

Haley struggled to keep her legs from shaking. "Just one question." She hugged herself tightly. "Please."

He locked his gaze on her, inches away.

She lowered her lashes. "Are you close with your brother?"

Sterling grabbed her shoulders and pulled her against his body, glaring down at her with his striking eyes. "If he were dead, I would know it. He's my twin. So nice fucking try."

"He isn't dead." She couldn't raise her voice above a whisper. "He was released."

"Then what the fuck are you getting at?"

Her face flamed hot at her own attempt to distract him. "I'm…curious about you."

Sterling settled his sparkling gaze on her lips. "You don't know who you're fucking with, little girl."

A shrill screech rang outside the gothic mansion. Sterling studied Haley's face as something struck the building, and the walls shuddered. Behind him, plaster and wood burst and a full-grown dragon crashed into the wide hallway.

Haley broke away from him and ran toward Ginger. Damian's dragon was supposed to be allegiant to him alone, but it had come to her beckoning command.

Ginger grabbed Haley's hand as they weaved through a crowd of squealing demons. "We have to find Emily."

Flames blazed through demons as the dragon scorched the large hall.

Haley led Ginger down a narrow corridor. "We need weapons."

"What about the fucking dragon?"

"I can't command that thing."

"Sure, you can. You brought it here, didn't you?"

"Come now, witches." A demon hobbled over to them. "Raden is ready for you."

Ginger knocked the demon's claws away from the knife on his belt and snatched it from him. She thrust it into his chest as a large monster loomed behind her.

Haley bolted past the creature, grasping Ginger's shoulders, and broke into a run. Demons lurked in every corner of the hall, and the girls retreated toward the dragon's territory. Dodging charred bodies on the black marble, Haley sprinted away from the winged reptile as it prowled through the corridor.

Shiny metal zipped by her cheek, and she spun as a sword stuck into the side of the dragon's giant upper jaw. Her mouth went slack at the sight, and she shuffled backward. Two demon guards grabbed hold of Ginger.

"I've been waiting for you." Raden's deep voice sent tremors through her body. Tall and terrifying, he sauntered closer to Haley, crowding her back toward the wounded creature. "Fetch my sword for me, witch."

The dragon stumbled, disoriented as blood gushed from its snout, and rested its chin on the floor. Haley's knees locked as she turned toward the creature.

Her mind went blank of any Trinnian commands she knew, and she walked stiffly forward. Its gaze pinpointed on her, but the enormous jaws remained closed.

Grasping the sword, she used all her might and pulled it free from the suffering creature. It spread its wings and towered over her with a bellowing roar. Her legs collapsed under her, and she dropped the blade, blocking her face as the dragon advanced.

It snapped its giant teeth just shy of her arm, and Haley screamed. She closed her hand around the sword as the reptile lunged.

Damian skidded in front of her and placed his hand on the dragon's bleeding nose. He spoke his demonic language in a breathless voice, and the creature slowly lowered its wings.

"The oracles predicted you'd bring an army to my door, nephew." Raden raised his arms at his sides. "Where are your soldiers?"

He straightened and ran a hand under his nose as his dragon limped backward and slumped into a heap.

Haley got to her feet, gripping Raden's sword, and Damian scanned her body.

He leaned around, checking her over. "Noah got a call from Ginger, but the phone cut out when that fucker took you. Did anyone hurt you?" He eyed the collar with a grimace.

"Damian!" Raden started forward, his black robes flowing as he walked. "Don't ignore me, boy."

"Answer me." Damian studied her throat as he unfastened the enchanted rope.

"I'm not hurt." Haley swallowed, hoarse from screaming.

He took the heavy sword from her and pressed a coin into her palm. "Take Ginger and get out of here."

"Emily's here too."

"I know. Noah's leading an attack downstairs. We'll get her." Damian stared into her eyes. "I've got this, angel."

Raden swung a tall battle-ax toward him, and steel clanged as Damian swiftly raised the sword. He shoved him back and struck Raden's bicep, slicing off a piece of flesh.

Snarling, Raden hit Damian across the face with the head of the ax, drawing blood, then bashed his face again.

"Haley, get the fuck out of here." Damian swept the blade low to the ground and wedged it into Raden's knee.

Mesmerized by the fight, she snapped awake at his command. The demons guarding the room had fled, and Ginger stood nearby, clutching a small knife. Outside the chamber, the mansion vibrated with sounds of battle. Feral screams and crashing metal.

As Raden swung the ax, Damian skirted the blade, then used the invisible force of his mind power and wrenched it out of his grip, flinging it across the room. He raised the sword and drove it through his uncle's chest.

Raden gurgled a cough. With the blade still in his heart, he burst forward and wrestled Damian onto the floor. He sank his teeth into Damian's shoulder and tore the sinewy muscle.

The sword's point protruded from Raden's back, and Damian gripped the handle, slicing it down through his torso.

"This is how you killed her, uncle." Damian's radiant eyes gleamed as Raden loosened his jaws. "Right in front of me." He flipped him onto his back and ripped the sword from Raden's gaping stomach as he stood. "She had to hold in her organs like you are now."

Blood spurted from Raden's mouth as he cackled. "Whose brand does your witch carry?" His upper lip curled as he struggled to lift his head. "She will always belong to me, Damian. Her body is marked as mine."

Damian turned away from him and wiped the dripping blood from his eye.

Haley's insides burned as bitter tears welled up. "I never belonged to you." Her golden heat blazed in her hands, and white light suddenly emanated all around her.

Raden sat upright, cradling his abdomen. His dark red eyes sent a stab of terror through her. "Is that what you think, witch?"

She glared back at him. The hatred she'd carried inside for so long surfaced as she thought of all the evil ways he'd violated her. Intense power surged inside her faster than she could control. Raden grinned as white and gold flames spread over his lower body. He climbed to his feet.

As Raden advanced, his skin melting, she focused her powers. Sparkling lights floated in the air around him as her magic fire engulfed him.

Damian moved in front of her and struck his blade above Raden's shoulders, severing his head.

Her stomach jolted at the sight, and she watched the flaming heap roll along the marble floor. Energy coursed through her limbs as her magic slowly diminished and the golden fire disappeared, leaving his slumped charred body.

Damian set down the sword and took her hand. His hands were dirty and bleeding as he opened her fingers. He touched the drakpiece still nestled there. "Take Ginger with you."

She nodded. Her legs felt numb, barely holding her upright.

Ginger watched the door with a blank expression, mascara smeared along her cheeks. Fighting still raged in the hallway as Adversus soldiers filtered into the chamber.

It wasn't the right time to express her deep emotion, but Haley leaned forward anyway. Damian vibrated with raw strength, and she threw her arms around his torso, nestling her face against him.

Noah grabbed hold of Ginger. He yanked up her bloodstained shirt and sank to his knees. "Fuck. You're okay." He pressed his forehead against her smooth stomach. "I'm so sorry, baby."

Haley tilted her face up. Damian's wounded shoulder had bled onto her skin. "What about Emily?"

"Emily was rescued." Noah got up and pulled Ginger close. "She's safe." He kissed her mouth.

Haley gripped Damian tightly in her arms. "Thank you."

"Sorry I couldn't accomplish it sooner." He cupped his hand around the back of her head and gave her an open-mouthed kiss, sweeping his tongue into her mouth, grazing it along hers, then pulled back, lowering his dark lashes as he focused on her lips. "Go to headquarters. Or home. You don't need to be here."

With a nod, she leaned up and gave him a tender kiss.

He had killed her tormentor. She'd carried the crippling fear for so many years, and Damian had set her free. She could finally let go.

CHAPTER TWENTY-ONE

Damian picked up a shot of whiskey as Stephen emptied the bottle into three more glasses.

"Oh, man." Noah grabbed one with a sigh. "I don't want to be wasted during my vows."

"I'm sure the girls are getting trashed right now too." Stephen lifted a glass. "Noah and Ginger."

The expensive liquor went down smoothly, and Damian set his empty glass on the table. Noah yanked on his tie again, readjusting it while Adam helped him with his cuff links.

Stephen twisted open a fresh bottle and kept pouring, glancing toward Damian. "You got your speech all set?"

Damian leaned down and grabbed a new drink. "Fuck no." Nobody had mentioned anything about a speech.

"You don't have a speech?" Stephen bent his neck forward. "You're the best man."

Noah chuckled. "I don't really give a shit about a speech, Hawthorne."

"Maybe I've been around my woman too much lately." Stephen broke into a smile. "Aimee practiced her maid of honor toast a hundred fuckin' times last night."

Damian looked up. "Is Haley giving one?" She didn't like to be in the spotlight, but she was also a maid of honor. Anything wedding-related seemed so crucial.

Stephen shrugged. "You'd know better than I would."

Haley hadn't been practicing anything as far as he knew. And she was most likely tired of explaining things to him. He felt like a fucking idiot every time the wedding subject came up.

"Ceremony starts in fifteen minutes." Adam gulped his drink and patted Noah's shoulder. "Ready to go up there?"

"Just about." Noah messed with his hair in front of the mirror. "You guys go meet the girls, I'll see you out there."

As the others meandered out of the room, Damian leaned against the dresser.

Noah looked him over with a grimace. "Damn, brother, you can wear a fucking suit." He glanced in the mirror and jerked the lapels on his jacket. "Making me look bad on my wedding day."

"Shut the fuck up." Damian took a long drink and put down the glass. "You need anything?"

Grinning, Noah scratched the back of his neck. "As long as she shows up, I'm good." He nodded toward the door.

"You nervous?" Damian followed him out.

He gave a confident shake of his head, but his energy vibrated with anxiety. They reached the back entrance to the stage and Noah blew out a breath.

"This is it." He twisted the knob, pausing with a thoughtful smile.

"Don't fuck up." Damian smiled as he walked away.

Noah laughed. "Fuck you."

Damian pushed his hands into his pockets and headed to the other side of the large venue. The ballroom where the ceremony would be held had to be packed. Hundreds of scattered thoughts rattled from the other side of the wall. A wedding was a special kind of torture.

The foyer was crowded with faces he didn't recognize. Noah's younger sister waved at him as he passed. The women beside her stared in his direction, and he caught a glimpse of their thoughts, revealing sexual desire toward him. He shouldered through a cluster of people.

Adam and Stephen sipped their drinks as they carried on a conversation with Noah's parents. A heavy black curtain separated the aisle, to be drawn when it was time to walk toward the altar. Haley stood next to it, holding a glass of champagne and talking with Aimee.

He took a seat on a bench across from her and leaned back, resting his hand on his leg. Her sapphire floor-length dress matched her eyes perfectly. She spotted him, and her red lips parted as she gave him a onceover.

Tucking her hair behind her ear, she diverted her attention back to Aimee. "Really? How do you know?"

"I just have this feeling. So, Noah proposed at Snoqualmie Falls, right?" Aimee clinked her champagne flute against Haley's and took a sip. "Beautiful place, and you have the weekend getaway at the lodge, it's great. But I told Stephen he should've done it while they were in Mexico. I mean, beach proposal? Gorgeous." She tapped Haley's arm. "So, Stephen's taking me to Puerta Vallarta this weekend."

"And you have a feeling..." Haley smiled, taking a drink of champagne.

"Yes! But hey, you think you could read his mind for me so I'd know for sure?"

Haley slipped her hand to her stomach as she giggled. "No."

"Why not?"

"Don't you want it to be a surprise?"

Aimee flipped her hand. "I hate surprises."

"It sounds like he's gonna propose."

"I guess I'm just gonna have to wait and see." Aimee stuck her tongue out, then took another drink. "I'll bet you peek on your own boyfriend's thoughts, though. When's he gonna propose?"

Her mouth fell open as she searched for a response. Damian sat up a little straighter on the bench.

Haley dropped her thick eyelashes with a trace of a smile. "I don't know if he's really that kind of boyfriend."

What the fuck did that mean?

"Well, you want him to propose, right?"

"I think he can hear us, he's right over there." Her cheeks turned a rosy color as she sipped her drink.

Unbelievable.

Haley eased back the edge of the curtain. "Holy fuck, there are a lot of people out there." She peered through the slit in the fabric. "I hope I don't trip." She tugged her dress down over her hips. "And then fall right on my face."

"Yeah, but who gives a fuck about any of these people?" Aimee gulped down most of her champagne.

Stephen came up behind Aimee and took away her glass. "It's about that time. Why aren't you girls with the bride?"

Damian got up and strolled toward them.

"She's taking a little time to pay respects to her dad." Aimee snagged her drink back from Stephen.

"She requested solitude." Haley straightened as Damian approached. "Hi."

"Hey." He couldn't help but lean in and kiss her scarlet lips, plump and sensual. Haley swallowed when he pulled back. He wanted more, but her brother was about a foot away.

She lowered her head and brushed her fingers along her lips. He imagined her smeared lipstick after sucking on him. Her feverish, wet mouth.

Classical music played at an increased volume, and everyone began to line up. Haley set her glass on a tray and slid her fingers through her hair.

"I won't let you fall." Damian offered her his arm.

With a trace of a smile, she wrapped her hands around his forearm and leaned her head against his bicep.

Ginger shuffled in front of him, a blur of white lace and silk, and whispered to Haley.

"How's my makeup?"

Haley let go of him and pressed her hands to her chest. "Beautiful, Ginge."

Aimee turned toward them. "Oh Christ, Ginger, you look fantastic." Tears gleamed in her eyes.

Haley didn't appear to be crying, but her eyes carried a bright sparkle. Stephen hooked his arm around Aimee's waist, and they walked out onto the aisle.

"We're next." Haley's voice trembled as she gathered her skirt and held onto his arm. She repositioned the flower tied to her wrist.

"Ready?" He forced his gaze away from her blushing chest.

"Yep." She drew up a handful of her dress and took a step. Her sky-high heels tangled in the silk and Damian gripped onto her as she lost her footing.

"You got this, angel?" He couldn't keep from smiling.

"Shit." Haley shook out her skirt. "Okay."

"We'll take it slow." He led her through the curtain.

Masses of wedding guests lined the aisle on both sides. Haley kept her focus on her shoes as they walked along the white runner.

"You want me to carry you?"

Her tensed posture loosened and she smiled up at him. Bright lights flashed from several angles as the crowd snapped dozens of pictures.

"I can make it."

At the end of the aisle, Haley clasped his hand tightly and didn't let go as she climbed the wide stairs in front of the stage. He escorted her to the top, and she caressed her thumb across his skin just before breaking the connection.

He took his place beside Noah on the opposite side, and the music changed. The ballroom came alive with cheers as Ginger emerged. She didn't take her eyes off Noah as she drifted down the aisle.

Damian suppressed the nagging thought that came to mind, bothered by the overheard conversation. For months, the same image had continued to haunt him. A fantasy of his girlfriend walking toward him in a white dress. But she didn't picture him as someone she could marry.

As Haley watched Noah and Ginger make their promises to each other, a tear rolled down her face. She brushed it away, and Aimee grasped her hand, wiping her own cheeks.

Noah and Ginger were pronounced husband and wife, and they proceeded back down the aisle together.

The party was already set up outdoors on the same property. The late afternoon sun illuminated the gardens surrounding them. Most of the guests headed down a busy pathway and Damian guided Haley toward a grassy field instead.

She held his hand as she wandered through the lush greenery with him. "I always cry during the vows. I can't help it."

He was glad it was over. "Sounds like we'll be going to Stephen's wedding next."

She swiveled toward him. "Did he say that?"

Damian didn't answer. *Fuck.* His stalker tendencies probably came off a little unsettling.

She paused. "You were listening?"

He kept quiet for a minute as they trekked through the meadow. "You said I'm not that kind of boyfriend."

"Well." Haley slowed her pace. "I just can't picture you… I mean, the whole wedding thing is not really you."

His heart wrenched in his chest. He hadn't been able to stop picturing it. "And that's what you want. A wedding, husband… All of this shit."

She lowered her chin and played with the white flower on her wrist. "Yeah, I do."

Just not with him. Damian halted, rubbing the back of his neck. "So you're gonna find someone who *is* the marrying kind. Someone more like Neil?" Shit, he was going off the rails.

"Neil?"

"I know you two talked about marriage."

"You don't actually believe I want to marry Neil."

"I know I'm an evil motherfucker, Haley." His chest constricted and he cleared his throat. "And when you said you were gonna become immortal?"

"If it's possible." She broke eye contact. "But…I don't want to lose myself doing it. Not like my uncle."

Damian tugged on his tie and unbuttoned his collar. "You don't need to become immortal if we're just fucking."

Her eyes flashed as tears surfaced, and she smacked her fist against his chest. "Why did you say that?" She hit him again, then jerked her skirt up, storming away from him.

He caught her arm, and she stiffened. Breaking free, she grasped between her heaving breasts.

Damian followed and closed his arms around her from behind. She hunched forward, but he held her tight.

"Calm down."

"We're just fucking?" Haley fought against his grip. "Don't touch me."

"No, we're not just fucking. That's the point."

She went limp in his arms and slumped onto the ground. Damian sat down, and she covered her face.

"I'm different with you, Haley." He touched her wrist, coaxing her to lower her hands. "I don't ever want this to end."

As she caught her breath, Haley closed her eyes and nodded.

They were alone in the meadow, and Damian's pulse jacked up as he moved his hand into his pocket. The timing was terrible, but he had reached a breaking point. He'd been carrying it with him for weeks, the tiny box that plagued him with restless thoughts.

He set it on her satin-covered knee. His heartbeat thudded as she stared at it for what felt like an eternity before she finally opened it.

"Marry me?"

She kept her gaze fixed on the vintage ring. A huge sapphire surrounded by diamonds. The jewel was deep blue, the color her eyes turned when they glittered at him in the dark, whenever she was desperate to come.

His stomach tightened into knots as the seconds rolled by.

"Say something."

"Yes." Haley gingerly slid the ring onto her finger. She tilted her left hand, and it sparkled in the light. "It's so…" Her voice caught, and she crawled onto his lap.

"I didn't plan it like this, I know it's supposed to be—"

Tears shined in her eyes as she planted her scarlet mouth on his, closing her arms around his neck.

He felt like he could breathe again, the weight lifted from his chest. He kissed her back and laid her down on the soft grass.

"I thought you hated this wedding stuff." She grasped his collar, drawing him closer.

"I still want to marry you."

Haley smiled. "Just a tiny wedding, I promise." She gazed up at him with incandescent eyes. "I love you."

His heart melted, and he pressed his face against her supple chest as she studied the ring. *I don't deserve to feel this good.*

She traced her nails along the back of his head. "We should keep it a secret for now."

"What?" He lifted his head and caught her gaze. "Why?"

"It's just not classy to announce it at someone else's wedding."

"Alright." He didn't care if anyone knew, as long as she was content with the idea of marrying him.

As they headed toward the party, Haley caressed the cluster of jewels on her finger. "How long have you had this?"

He glanced downward. "Couple months."

Her mouth dropped open. "That's a long time."

"I was nervous, I guess."

Haley leaned against him as they approached the bustling crowd. "I think this is the happiest day of my life."

* * *

It was nearly midnight when they arrived home after the reception. Damian unclasped his watch and opened the sliding door in their bedroom, letting in the summer night breeze. Beside the bed, Haley fidgeted with her zipper. He stripped out of his shirt and tie as she slid off her high heels, still struggling behind her back.

"Here." Damian took over for her. The tiny closure wouldn't budge without breaking.

Haley felt her stomach. "I think I need to do some sit-ups."

He covered her hands with his over her soft belly. "I think it's cute." His heart raced at the feeling of his ring on her finger. He moved his palms upward, groping her tits through the satin, and her nipples stiffened. He pulled the fabric into his fists and yanked it apart.

Haley gasped as he pulled the dress away from her naked body. She never wore any fucking panties anymore. His dick throbbed as he leaned around and caught her breast in his mouth. Full and sweet, he groaned at the taste. Haley trailed her fingers down between her thighs, and he grasped her wrist.

"You don't touch yourself unless I tell you to." Damian pulled her hands behind her. "Do I need to tie you up?"

Haley nodded. With a smirk, he bent her forward. She rested her cheek on the plush comforter while he slid the drawer open. He wrapped a smooth rope around her thighs, binding them together, and knotted it. Holding her wrists with one hand, he lifted her onto the bed with the other.

On her knees, she buried her face in the blanket, bending forward with her ass in the air, displaying her beautiful sex for him. Damian kept her hands pinned to her lower back and moved onto the bed.

"I'm gonna spank you, naughty girl." He ran his rough palm along her pussy, and she took a sharp breath. "Say please."

Haley tilted her face toward him. "Please, Master."

Damian slapped her ass, and she moaned into the bed. *Such a sexy, filthy girl.* He spanked her again and dragged his fingertips over the heated skin. She purred for him, and he lost himself in the sound.

He slowly caressed her pussy lips with a light touch, and she squirmed a little. He teased her helplessly exposed clitoris with his calloused fingers, tormenting her until she was breathless and trembling.

He loosened the rope around her legs and released her wrists.

"I want your sweet mouth all over my cock."

Haley hurriedly opened his belt. She grazed her tongue along his ab muscles as she lowered his zipper.

Jerking his boxer briefs down, she took his length into her greedy mouth.

Pleasure flooded through his groin, and he gathered her silky curls in his fist. "Are you still gonna suck me like this when you become my wife?"

Her response was a deep moan as his tip touched the back of her throat. He pulled back, and she licked her lips, her eyes glittering up at him. "Yes."

Damian picked up the rope and tied it in a knot around her wrists in front of her. He slid the rope along the headboard, then laid her back and secured her arms above her. "Be a good girl and spread your legs wide for me."

Biting her full bottom lip, she opened them. She was glistening wet for him. He ran his fingers up her inner thigh, and Haley parted her lips, watching him.

He tied her legs taut to each bedpost and moved on top of her. His loose belt buckle dragged against her exposed pussy, and she tensed.

"I'm always gonna be your master, Haley." He held one side of her throat as he kissed along her jawline and pressed his groin against her. "Even when I'm your husband."

She took quiet, fast breaths. "Please make love to me, Master."

Hardening to the point of pain, he shoved his pants down and kicked them off. Haley's sultry gaze slid along his naked body.

The ropes held her legs wide apart, and Damian sank his cock in deep. "Ugh, fuck, you feel so good."

She clenched around his dick as he drew out of her, sending him to a new height of desire.

He forced himself to slow down, entering her at an agonizingly slow pace. "Tell me you love me."

Haley writhed against her ropes. "I love you, Damian."

A chill tickled the back of his neck, and he looked back at the dark shadow at the foot of their bed.

His father ripped him apart from her and slammed him against the wall. Damian slid to the floor. Lucifer stretched his wings and climbed onto the bed, kneeling between her legs.

Damian's heart thundered in his chest as he fought the choking grip of his father's dark power, but he couldn't move.

CHAPTER TWENTY-TWO

Haley swallowed, gasping for breath as Lucifer traced the sharp point of his claw along her branded stomach.

"Did you think you got away with it, witch?"

"Father." Damian sounded more desperate than she'd ever heard him, and her eyes stung with tears. "Take me instead. Please."

"You can handle physical torture rather well, son." Lucifer stared down at her pussy, still tingling from Damian's attention, and her body went rigid. "It's when the witch is threatened that you crumble and break. I will break you, Damian." His forked tongue slithered between his lips.

"I'm gonna fucking murder you." Damian jerked against the oppressive darkness holding him in place.

"Not before I peel her skin back." His face hovered over hers. His lizard-like red eyes and monstrous fangs sent a jolt of terror through her. She held back a scream, her pulse racing.

Damian growled an inhuman sound. "Don't fucking touch her."

"It's okay, baby." Haley swallowed harshly. "I'm alright."

She grasped onto the rope binding her wrists and beckoned her powers.

Lucifer sneered, revealing his razor teeth. "I'm going to bite off her clitoris, Damian. We'll see how well she's doing then."

He dipped his head toward her painfully exposed sex, and a choked scream escaped Haley's throat.

Blinding white light illuminated the entire room, and Haley winced. She blinked as another presence drifted toward her, bathed in ethereal light.

"Grace." Staring at Haley's mother, Lucifer sat back on his heels, his wings retracting. "I knew you would come."

Haley's mind went fuzzy, unable to process what she was seeing. She looked exactly as she did when Haley was ten years old. Long auburn curls and delicate features. The powerful glow exuded from her body, draped in white silk.

"I was very specific when I terminated your ludicrous contract regarding my daughter's life. Neither you or Raden were to ever harm her again."

"I needed to see you."

Haley focused her golden heat on the rope above her and freed her wrists.

Grace fixed her gaze on Haley. "Come with me, sweetheart."

Blinking her eyes, Haley tried to comprehend what her mother was asking.

"You cannot ignore me, witch. I will destroy your sons next."

"Then I will destroy yours." Grace's blue eyes shone with an icy fire. She pointed her finger at Damian. "You can have your heir. I will bring Haley with me to the afterworld."

"And the other heir?" Lucifer moved off the bed and loomed over Grace. "What will become of that one?"

"The spawn will not exist in the After-Place."

"Please don't leave." Lucifer reached for her, and she swerved his touch.

His father's hold broke, and Damian got to his feet. He rushed to the bed and worked on the rope around Haley's ankle, fumbling to open the knot with jerking fingers.

"No." Grace advanced toward him. "You've done enough to my little girl."

Damian straightened and stepped back from her.

"You're the one who restrained her with these disgusting ropes." Grace waved her fingers, and the knots fell apart. "I'm setting her free from you."

Grace's hateful tone tore into Haley's heart. "Mother, don't speak to him that way." She climbed to her knees, folding her arms to shield herself.

Grace shifted her glare from Damian and extended her hand toward Haley. "You've been through too much at the hands of their wicked family, dear. It's time to join your father and me in our afterlife."

"Who is the other heir?" Damian looked at his father.

Lucifer gave a grating laugh. "I suppose you'll never know, son."

Damian's gaze flashed to Grace. "Tell me."

Grace clenched her fists. "You can return to Hell where you belong, Damian."

Haley's heartbeat crashed in her chest. "Please don't talk to him like that."

"Who is the heir?" Damian stared at Grace. "Who is it?"

"That monster will never see the light of day." She reached toward Haley again. "Come, dear."

"No…" Haley barely felt the tears streaming down her face. "I won't leave him."

Grace shook her head and held onto her chest. "Damian is evil. The spawn inside you is a demonic creature, just like him. Just like Lucifer."

Her lungs froze as chills crawled through her entire body. She touched her stomach.

"Fuck." Damian buried his face in his hands.

Grace floated past him. "You can leave all this pain behind."

Haley gripped her belly with both hands. She gasped as a wave of emotion overwhelmed her. "How could you say that about our child?"

"It isn't a child, darling. It's a spawn of the devil. He'll one day become the ruler of Hell."

A baby boy was growing inside her. Damian's child. Their little one's future couldn't be decided already.

"No. We'll raise him properly."

Damian glanced up and caught her gaze.

"Right, baby?" She looked into Damian's thoughts and found them shrouded in darkness.

"Haley Grace." Her mother clasped her shoulder. "You cannot raise a deformed creature with this monster you've grown so attached to."

The firm addition of her middle name raised a familiar pang of guilt, but Haley kept her focus on Damian. With a troubled look, he held her gaze and nodded.

A calmness washed over her, and she turned to Grace. Her heart broke at the sight of her mother, and she climbed off the bed. "I didn't realize it was you who saved us at Aunt Collette's house… Thank you." As tears flooded her eyes, she embraced her mother, somehow saturated with tranquility despite the horrific monster hovering a few feet away.

"I didn't intend to rescue Damian." Grace pulled back from her. "But I couldn't let him control your existence like that. Changing your entire reality after his uncle split you open with that wretched knife he gave you."

"Damian killed Raden, mother. His own uncle."

Lucifer's sullen silence seemed to carry a cold electricity.

"Yes, he murdered *your* uncle as well." She snapped her gaze toward Damian. "My brother."

"Uncle Eli had become a monster." Haley withdrew from her mother and stood in front of Damian.

Damian grabbed a pair of boxer briefs from a drawer and handed her one of his T-shirts.

"My brother had his faults, but he did not deserve to die at the hands of Lucifer's spawn."

Time slowed as Haley slid on the T-shirt. She clutched her stomach. "Eli sold me to Raden."

"And Raden is the spawn's uncle. You cannot—"

"Stop calling him that!" Her voice took on a deep desperation. "He's my family."

"Hey." Behind her, Damian held his strong arms around her. He brought his mouth to her ear. "You don't need to get upset for me, okay?" He grasped her belly through the T-shirt, and butterflies flitted through her.

Grace brushed away a tear and pushed her thick hair behind her shoulder. "My sweet daughter. The devil has his claws in so deep."

Lucifer chuckled softly. "This is thrilling news for you, Damian? The deformed creature who will tear your witch apart from the inside?"

Damian's muscles went rigid, and he let go of her stomach.

"His spawn is going to kill you, Haley. It's what I'm here to save you from." Her mother grabbed her hands, and Haley flinched.

"I'm not going with you." She pulled away, swiveling toward Damian and caught a glistening tear in his eye before he glanced away. The sight struck her motionless for a moment. Her whispering voice turned shaky. "I'm not going anywhere. Please don't ask me to, baby."

He lowered his head and rubbed his brow. "I want you to be safe."

Haley took his palm and held it against her stomach. "I'm strong enough for whatever's coming. You know I am."

He drew in a breath.

Grace stepped between them and slipped her hands to Haley's cheeks. "He is—"

"No." Haley moved backward. "Please stop." Her vision clouded as she tried to fight the tears welling up. "I'm never gonna leave him, mother. If you knew him, you'd understand." She clasped her chest as her breath caught. "He's so easy to love."

Grace closed her eyes and tilted her chin down. "I can't protect you from yourself." She raised her hand in Lucifer's direction, cloaking him in a sea of light until he vanished. "This abomination growing inside you *will* destroy your human body."

Haley slid her arms around her middle. The desire to protect their little one outweighed the stab of fear.

"You aren't concerned about that?" Grace gave her a pointed look.

"I am." Haley tried to steady her legs. "It's worth the risk."

Damian grunted. "We need to talk about this, Haley."

She glanced at his tormented expression, then shifted her attention to Grace. Her mother's death had brought her so much agonizing loss, and it had shadowed her entire life. She'd dreamed of the moment she could speak to her again.

And now, she had a new family.

"I'm having this child."

Grace let out a small cry as her brows crinkled together. "My baby girl is so lost." She pressed her lips together and nodded. "If this is your choice, Haley Grace, you will live with this decision for eternity, is that understood?"

Haley moved closer to Damian and leaned against his firm body. She forced herself to breathe, wrapping her arms around him, and nodded. "I choose him."

Grace reached forward and grazed a light touch along Haley's cheek. An intense heat spread through her body.

Haley jolted and looked down, grasping her stomach as the warmth enveloped her entirely. "What did you do?" she cried out. "Please don't hurt my baby."

"I have made you immortal." Grace spoke in a flat, monotone voice. "If you insist on destroying yourself, at least you won't end up like your uncle." She shot a glare toward Damian. "Gone into the black abyss. No Hawthorne ever belongs there."

Stunned, Haley looked down at her hands as the strange heat escaped her palms.

"Your body will remain at this age for eternity. Your wounds will heal almost immediately." She sighed. "At least you'll have a fighting chance when you attempt to give birth to that filthy monster." A bright light flashed through the room, and Grace disappeared with it.

Silence fell over the darkened room. Damian sank onto the bed.

Driven by curiosity, Haley hurried to the nightstand and yanked open the top drawer. Damian watched as she sliced an enchanted knife point along her forearm. Blood rushed from the gash just before her skin mended. She set the knife down with a quivering hand, numbed by the emotions rushing through her. Her mind had gone blank.

He pulled her toward him by her wrist and ran his thumb through the blood, studying the small mark on her skin. With a thoughtful look, he grasped the bottom of the T-shirt and glided it up and over her head. The branded R still adorned her belly. Flattening his palm against her stomach, Damian drew her onto his lap.

His body heat soothed her, and Haley nudged her forehead against his throat, resting in his sturdy hold. She had so much to lose now. The sense of impending doom invaded her thoughts.

"Do you think Lucifer wants our little boy to be the dark lord?" she asked.

"My father will never get near us again." The fierce edge in his tone set her nerves at ease.

She closed her eyes. Whatever dangers lurked ahead, they could weather the storm.

The purest emotion reflected through his touch as he caressed her scarred stomach with his large hand. "I'll do whatever it takes to keep you both protected."

Tears blinded her. Her mother's remarks weighed heavily on her chest, and she looked down at the shimmering jewel he'd given her. Her attentive, loving man didn't deserve the horrid things Grace had said about him. He was the love of her life, and the fact that Grace despised him tainted Haley's view of her. She resolved to focus instead on the kind, gentle woman she remembered from her childhood, when her mother was still flesh and blood, not an otherworldly spirit being.

Damian picked her up and moved her to the middle of the bed. As she sank her head into the pillow, she circled her arms around his neck, pulling him on top of her.

"Your mother…" he muttered softly.

Haley caught his somber gaze.

Glancing away, he shifted off of her and rested his head on the pillow beside her. "She's right about me."

His soft-spoken words made her heart ache. "She's not." Facing him, she held her palm against his cheek. "She doesn't know you. If she was still alive, she'd love you, I know it." She traced her fingertip along his jawline, lowering her voice. "You're my family, Damian. You're all I need."

He kept silent for a moment, gazing into her eyes. "Forever's a long time."

"I know." She snuggled closer to him. "You're mine for eternity."

He pulled up the corner of his mouth as he brushed a lock of cinnamon hair away from her face, gliding his fingers through the long strands. "You sure you want me for that long?"

Lost in his deep green eyes for a moment, she nodded.

He leaned toward her and hovered his mouth in front of hers. "Good," he whispered, then gently pressed his soft lips to hers.

She swept her thumb along his cheek, and he deepened his kiss, sliding his demanding tongue along hers.

Damian broke the kiss. "You belong with me, angel."

Her heartbeat fluttered, and her lips spread into a smile.

He drifted his gaze down to her stomach and skimmed his knuckles against her scar. "Are you afraid of what's coming?"

"You mean our little one?" Her voice came out soft.

He glanced into her eyes. "Yeah."

An overwhelming peace flowed through her at the thought of their creation. Haley could suddenly feel Damian's presence in her thoughts, and she shook her head, biting her bottom lip. "Are you?"

He studied her mouth for a moment. "No. Like you said, we can handle whatever's coming."

Tingling warmth permeated through her chest. His love seemed to make her stronger. They had a frightening road ahead of them, but she could endure anything with him at her side.

Haley slipped her palm along his rough whiskers. "We should probably get married soon since I'm only gonna get bigger…" She looked down at herself and lowered her hand to her belly. "It might make for an uncomfortable honeymoon."

Caressing his fingers along her scarred skin, he studied her stomach with a handsome smile. "I like the idea of you growing heavy with our child."

Filled with effervescence, Haley relaxed into the pillow.

She still wanted to look hot in her wedding dress though, and have insanely kinky sex with her new husband on their wedding night…

She felt Damian lingering inside her head, witnessing her X-rated thoughts.

He pulled her closer, his eyes flickering in amusement. "I guess we better start planning this thing, Mrs. Pierce."

~ About the Author ~

Savannah Hill writes romance and has a weakness for cupcakes and protective book heroes. She loves nature, heavy metal music, and is pretty much obsessed with deep, true love. She lives in the beautiful Pacific Northwest.

www.ingramcontent.com/pod-product-compliance
Lightning Source LLC
Chambersburg PA
CBHW071307170626
46809CB00001B/353